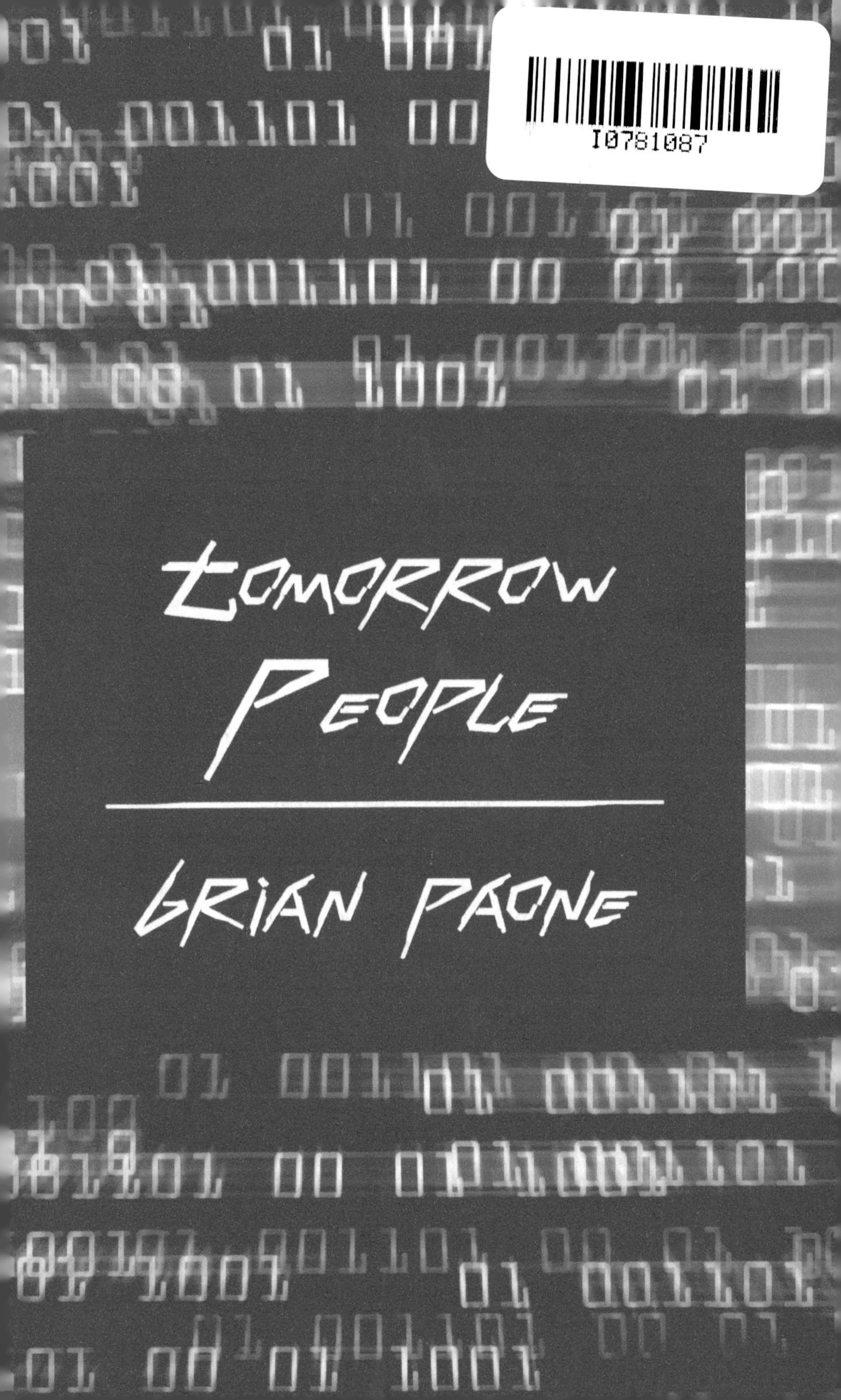

tomorrow
People
Brian Paone

Dedicated to all Billy Idol fans who thought *Cyberpunk* was an amazing album.

Editor: Denise Barker
Graphic Designer & Author Photo: Amy Hunter
Copyeditor: Gerri Rodriguez
Formatter: Kari Holloway

Published by Scout Media
Copyright 2024
ISBN (print): 978-1-960855-07-7
ISBN (eBook): 978-1-960855-08-4

September 14, 2023 — August 12, 2024
(Fort Belvoir, VA / Fort Leonard Wood, MO / Waynesville, MO /
Saint Robert, MO)

For more information on my books and music:
www.BrianPaone.com

1

"Do you want to be hypnotized?" the man asked. An orange leather mask covered his face, and torn and tattered strips of orange cloth hung from his orange shirt and pants.

The woman lying on the metal table wondered if the man had cut his clothes to look more sinister or whether his clothes had been frayed from years of living in this desolate, orange-tinged landscape.

The man peered at the woman for her answer, his eyes peeking through dust- and grime-covered goggles. She could barely see his orange pupils through the muck covering the lenses.

The woman ran her tongue across her front teeth to steady herself before making a final decision. She surveyed the room, hesitating before replying. Everything was orange from either dust or dirt. Computer screens covered almost every inch of wall space, each haphazardly hung so they tilted in their unique way, not even one hung level. Two monitors rested on wheeled stands, one keeping track of her heart rate and the other? Well, she didn't know what the other's purpose was.

"*Hrm?*" he asked, impatient, standing over the table.

She held her breath and didn't like that the only door in the room was closed. She felt trapped, stifled, claustrophobic. But that was why she was here in the first place, right? She wanted what this man could give her. She wanted to be free of this plane of existence. She wanted to peacefully move into whatever afterlife his special trancing promised.

Into whatever magic this stranger, dressed head-to-toe in raggedy orange garb, had promised her.

These were the neuro-trancers—the wizards in these wastelands. They were to be feared and respected and adored, all at the same time. And this man boasted to be one of the most revered of the neuro-trancers.

"I do want to be hypnotized," she squeaked out.

The man handed her a small keypad. "Please transfer all your credits. This is your donation to Mother Dawn and your payment for the service."

The woman swallowed hard, entered her credit identification number, then hit Transfer. Everything she owned now belonged to the neuro-trancers. With her account completely emptied—the so-called donation to the Mother Dawn deity—he could now continue.

The man nodded and grabbed a large syringe from a metal table next to the monitor tracking her heart rate.

"Will it hurt?" she asked.

He paused and tilted his head at her. "No more than the pain we endure in this life. Then you'll get the happiness you deserve."

She swallowed hard and nodded just once.

He approached her, lifted the shirt sleeve on her left arm, and brought the needle toward the exposed flesh.

"Wait! How …" She cleared her throat. "How fast does it take?"

He paused, the large needle containing an orange fluid leveled at her forearm. "You will be trancing before I even stop pushing the plunger. You can try to count before it takes effect, but I have never had anyone reach *three*."

With her index finger, she scratched an itch at her hairline. "Okay." She took a deep breath in and held it for a second, then blew it all out. "Let's do it."

His orange-gloved hand holding the needle now moved toward her again. The tip pushed into her skin, making an indent, then poked through the surface. "Praise Mother Dawn."

She inhaled through her clenched teeth, waiting for either pain or bliss—she wasn't sure which to expect—and mumbled her response, "Mother Dawn be praised."

The orange-soaked room swirled in her vision. Dots and hues of pastel colors she had only heard about in stories invaded her sight. Yellows and greens and baby blues and lavender superimposed over the orange room.

Until the room was gone.

Orange was gone. Dust and dirt and grime were gone. Then more colors than she even knew could possibly exist exploded around her, and she exploded with them, becoming a singularity with them, as she winked out of existence.

The trancing was completed. And there was no returning. The neuro-trancer had saved her, had removed her pain and suffering, and, for all her worldly assets, had awarded her with a one-way ticket to the only afterlife so many people believed in anymore.

Right here. In a place they could only refer to as Shangri-la.

Adam sat on a trail rail in the empty subway tunnel, hunched over a metal trinket he had found earlier in the week, a tiny screwdriver in hand, a monocle covering his right eye. He scrunched his eyebrows to concentrate, closing his left eye so his right eye could focus clearer through the magnifying lens. He used the screwdriver to try to pry off the center tab that connected three circles.

"Need some company?" Adam's best friend, Jonesy, slid into a sitting position next to him.

"I wish I knew what this was." Adam pinched the center of the orange item between his thumb and index finger and spun it. His voice echoed through the empty train tunnel without ricocheting, proving the bottomlessness of the dark corridor.

Jonesy took the item from Adam's hands and studied it. "You find this during the last raid?"

Adam nodded and adjusted his position on the metal train rail to alleviate some uncomfortableness in his buttocks. "Same time Maggie found that old gun."

"Did she bring the gun back?"

Adam chortled. "You haven't seen her wearing it every day in her waistband?"

Jonesy shook his head but smirked.

Adam smiled too. Maggie's childlike wonderment when finding new things seemed to help remind them all that they were still young, even if they were fighting an adult's battle against the megacorporations.

"I haven't seen her toting a gun, but that doesn't surprise me. She wearing it like those people in the Wild West in those history books of yours?"

"Pretty much spot-on. If she could find herself one of those horse animals that used to exist, she would be a rootin' tootin' cowgirl for sure."

"I … don't even know the words coming out of your mouth," Jonesy said with a chuckle.

The cold and dark train tunnel had proven to be a wealth of supplies and magical discoveries. They had pilfered so many items from the abandoned railway cars, items people once owned—from a time so long ago that those people just may as well be dinosaurs at this point.

Adam leaned his elbows onto his knees, while flipping the trinket through his fingers. "I don't think it's a worship device. Doesn't look like it has any circuitry or electrical components," Adam said.

"Not everything was electronic in the Age of Destruction. This might be something as simple as a child's toy."

Adam guffawed. "Could you imagine living in a time where we would have things to just play with, that served no other purpose than enjoyment? What a crazy time that must have been to live in."

Jonesy patted Adam's knee, then swiped a clump of long black hair from over his eyes to behind his ear. "You have an unhealthy obsession with the days of the ancients. You know that, right?"

Adam slid the monocle from his bright blue eyes and gazed at Jonesy. "Is it unhealthy to want to learn about a time that only left us relics and no concrete descriptions of how life was for them? Doesn't that intrigue you? That people lived right here, where we live now, so long ago, and the planet was so incredibly different?"

Jonesy ran his hands along the orange fabric of his pants, then clapped once, sending the sound down the tunnel and into the void of darkness. "I'm more intrigued at how we will eventually bring Cyber-Corp to its knees and restore the government to its rightful power."

Adam chuckled and moved his legs underneath him so he could stand. "See? You are a romantic as well. The only difference between us is that I romanticize about the people of the past." He proffered a hand to help his friend get to his feet. "And you romanticize about the people of the future."

"Well, none of this romanticizing will finish cooking the stew, so I gotta get back to making dinner."

They pulled themselves from the tracks and onto the subway platform. Ahead, Adam saw the moving silhouettes of their clan—a small band of renegades, misfits, rebels even, who had vowed to put a kink in Cyber-Corp's distribution of their Synchestria Implants. The only price that came with trying to take down the largest megacorporation in the hemisphere was that hired assassins would do anything to stop them.

0110000111111000111011100

Venus watched Adam return to their main living area on the subway platform, with Jonesy splitting off to finish cooking. She squinted to decipher what Adam carried. She believed it was the trinket he had found on their last raid on the railway cars farther down the tunnel. A smirk touched the left side of her mouth when she thought how childlike Adam could still be, even though they were all approaching their twenties. She found it hard to believe they were almost halfway through their life expectancy. She thought it a cruel joke, that just when they felt like adults and were graduating from their teens, they were already cresting the hill of a normal lifespan.

If Mother Dawn turned out to be a real, tangible entity—and not some fabled deity that the elders had concocted to keep everyone in line—Venus would have choice words for Mother Dawn about the unfairness of how short their time was on Earth. Venus had heard that the ancients had lived until eighty, ninety, and sometimes over one hundred years old. There was no proof of course—just anecdotes passed down through the centuries—but she found it wondrous, if not improbable.

Their small band of cyberpunks—at least that's what Cyber-Corp had dubbed them—bustled around Venus as she stood still, waiting for Adam to reach her. She slid the twine from her ponytail, ran her fingers through her hair, then resecured the ponytail, hoping she had captured any rogue wispies. Her heart pattered when Adam stopped in front of her.

"Baffled, I tell ya. I'm baffled." He handed Venus the trinket.

She flipped it over in her hands, her eyes like slits. "I haven't seen anything like this in any of the books we have found." She raised her gaze to meet his. "Why do you care so much about this anyway?"

He gently removed the item from her fingers and stared at it. "It signifies how much we still don't know about the ancients."

"And that ignorance is driving you crazy," she said with a playful smile.

"Driving me batshit crazy, as I think they used to say in old-speak."

Venus chuckled and beheld his ice-blue eyes. It was the one attribute that separated Adam from everyone else she had ever met. In her nineteen years, she had only ever seen orange eyes on a human. In fact, nobody she knew could remember meeting anyone with anything other than orange eyes.

Adam ran a hand through his moppy black hair and tugged on his orange vest to straighten it. "Maybe it's futile. I dunno. I just hate not knowing what the ancients used something for."

Venus interlaced her fingers into his and turned him so they could walk across the platform and toward the cooking area. The band of deviants—cyberpunks—had commandeered an ancient office as a firepit haven for cooking and heating water for bathing. Inside the office, Jonesy was on his haunches, dipping a row of freshly killed rodents on a large stick into a large pot of stew, resting over the licking flames.

"Smells good, man," Adam said and strode past the firepit. "Are any tea leaves left?"

Jonesy leaned back and pointed. "I think so, in that box."

Adam found a few leaves that didn't smell pungent, crumpled them in his fist, and dropped them into a mason jar, ready to add hot water once the firepit was free. "You want some?" he asked Venus.

She shook her head. "Maybe after dinner." She focused on the tall, lanky teen cooking their supper. "Making my mouth water, Jonesy."

The scent of the charring rodents made Adam's stomach growl with anticipation.

01100001111110001110111100

Happenstance had piecemealed together the band of six cyberpunks during the last few months. Only Venus and Adam and Jonesy had known each other prior to the group solidifying. They all sat in a circle, eating Jonesy's gourmet meal. Sounds of slurping and munching wafted down the dark tunnel to the left and to the right of the platform, not echoing the sounds back to them. Long-forgotten LED lights were still operational and illuminated the platform and what constituted as their *home*.

Cherie reclined with her palms behind her, while stretching her legs in front of her. She used the tip of her tongue to dislodge a piece of rodent meat between her two front teeth. "I still don't know why we aren't gonna hit the factory tomorrow. Let's just light it up and watch it burn."

Adam side-eyed her without moving his head. "We don't have enough intel on the structure. After a few more missions inside, then I'll be comfortable."

Venus grinned at Adam's leadership role. None of the six had picked a leader verbally, but Adam had inserted himself into the alpha role through his steadfast demeanor of not wavering when he thought he knew best. And the rest of them seemed to just fall in line behind him, like puppies.

Cherie rubbed her dirty palms on her orange pants and rose. "I'm gonna turn in. No sense talking about this. Not like I can get you to change your mind." She disappeared into a dark office, doubling as her bedroom, then stuck just her head out the doorway. "For what it's worth, I think waiting just gives Cyber-Corp the time it needs to completely dismantle what remnants we have left of a government. Then where will we be, Adam?"

Adam shrugged, unfazed by her hyperbole.

Mony shook her head. "For someone who despises authority, she sure doesn't give you too much of a fight."

Venus chortled and put her palm against her lips to stifle any further noise. She knew when Cherie was really worked up, any snickering sent in her direction could very quickly turn into exchanging blows with the gruff teenager.

Maggie used her hands to sign, asking what Cherie had said, as she hadn't seen Cherie's lips to read them.

Mony signed back, relaying the conversation.

Maggie nodded her acknowledgement, then shook her head in disagreement of Cherie's attitude, spinning her index finger next to her temple to indicate how she thought Cherie was crazy.

Mony signed to ask if Maggie wanted any more dinner, and she declined. Mony rose, patted Maggie's shoulder, and headed toward her own office-turned-bedroom.

"I think that's a great idea," Adam said, resuming his inspection of his new toy as he spun it. "Maybe we should all turn in."

Jonesy began the process to snuff out the fire and to collect the uneaten food. He gave a halfhearted salute to Adam. Upon his way to retire to his makeshift bedroom, he glanced at Maggie's back and recognized the small bulge under her shirt. He chuckled to himself. He hadn't noticed it before and silently applauded Maggie for keeping her newfound gun relic so discreet. They all deserved to have their own little joys, especially if it made them happy in such a desolate time.

Venus followed Adam into his living space and sighed heavily.

"A credit for your thoughts," Adam said while stripping off his shirt.

"I know Cherie can be a little too spontaneous for comfort"—she took his hands into hers—"but, if you remember, the first debate is next week."

Adam squinted at her, unsure what she was implying.

"A new president, voted in by those higher-ups at Cyber-Corp, just puts law and order further down the priority and gives the megacorporations more power to data-collect and to control."

Adam stepped backward but didn't release his hold on her hands. "So, you think we should strike the factory to disrupt the election process? Even if we don't truly know the ins and outs of the property?"

Venus bit her bottom lip. She knew she had to be delicate here choosing the right words to get Adam to understand how dire this situation might get. "Destroying millions of Synchestria Implant microchips would set Cyber-Corp back months and might be just enough to tip the scales on Election Day."

Adam ran his hand through his shaggy hair and pierced her with his ice-blue eyes. "Cyber-Corp is too powerful. Democracy is dead. The megacorporations pick the president. You know that. The polls are just to keep face. None of those votes actually matter."

Venus stepped toward him. "For Mother Dawn's sake, do you really believe that? Because, if you do, then what are we doing here? Why are we outlaws? Why not just join the population above"—she pointed ceilingward—"and sell our souls to the devil, like everyone else?"

"Not everyone." He narrowed his gaze at her. "Only the weak-minded."

"That's where you are wrong, Adam." She pointed at his chest. "The poor. The hopeless. The trapped. Those are who have been targeted. That doesn't make them weak-minded. They truly believe they are doing what's best for themselves and their family. It's commendable."

Adam chuckled and grabbed his new toy to spin it with his two fingers. "Commendable to allow Cyber-Corp to surgically insert an implant into your brain, that records and transmits to them everything you see, touch, taste, hear, and even feel? Purely for the sake of data-collecting?"

"Commendable to do whatever it takes to put food on the table and a roof over your head. I don't blame the population for taking the handout. People aren't the enemy here. I blame Cyber-Corp for creating such an evil method to line those people's pockets with enough credits to care for their families."

He delicately placed both hands on her forearms. "The Synchestria Implants are evil. You know that. They are using our own actions, opinions, and thoughts against us. And I don't think it's purely for marketing's sake or to *make our lives more fulfilling by giving us what we didn't know we needed.* I think it's more ..." He paused and looked down.

Venus spun to face him. "More, what?"

"More dangerous than that. World War Six dangerous. Information is currency. What happens when Cyber-Corp becomes the wealthiest entity in the world? And not monetarily. Wealthier than the superpowers of the world. Do you want a megacorporation running the free world? I don't. And that's why more and more ragtag teams of us so-called cyberpunks are springing up all over the country."

Venus nodded, knowing he was right. "Do you really think if there are enough of us, we can make a real difference?"

"If we keep growing as a movement, and if those other teams take it as seriously as we do and actually act upon it, I think we have a fighting chance to put the power back into the government's hands."

From the doorway, Jonesy asked, "Why would we want the old government back in power? Their poor management got the country to the poverty level it did, where we were so destitute that Cyber-Corp swooped into a position to run the country." He stepped into their room. "Didn't mean to eavesdrop, but don't you think getting rid of both Cyber-Corp and the old government should be synonymous so we can usher in a completely new and improved governing body?"

Adam and Venus remained silent.

Jonesy raised one hand and lowered his head in apology. "Sorry, sorry. I'll let you guys be. Just food for thought, ya know?" He headed off.

Adam studied his new trinket and pursed his lips.

"A credit for *your* thoughts?" Venus asked.

Adam nodded without raising his gaze at her. "Let's hit the factory tomorrow."

Venus smiled and pumped her fists ever-so-slightly at her sides so he wouldn't notice.

"Cherie must never think I changed my mind just because it was her idea," he said sternly.

Venus touched her fingertip to his nose. "I'll make sure everyone knows I convinced you."

Adam's smile spread ear to ear. "I honestly feel like that is the most believable scenario anyway." His smile turned into a devilish grin. "Can I convince you to stay with me tonight?"

She surrendered to his request, getting lost in those exotic ice-blue eyes.

3

Mr. Broad squinted and moved his chin slightly to the right. He spotted the silhouettes of bodies sleeping in the subway offices on the tele-skin that covered the entire back wall of his Cyber-Corp office. A small camera drone had entered the platform to do a sweep for cyberpunk cells hidden within the city. He pushed the tip of his tongue against one of his front teeth and smoothed his orange three-piece suit with one hand. The only item not orange in his ensemble was the gold chain that connected his pocket watch from a belt loop to the inside pocket of his jacket—a cracked pocket watch that didn't keep proper time, the second hand eternally stuck, clicking forward, then clicking backward, then repeat.

Mr. Broad spoke into the room. "Lancelot, get Johnny Ray on the line."

A computerized male voice responded from hidden speakers in the walls, "Yes, sir."

Mr. Broad stepped closer to the tele-skin on the far wall and focused on the six stationary figures. When Johnny Ray pushed through the office door, as if something were chasing him, Mr. Broad turned only his head. That man didn't know how to do anything slowly, Mr. Broad thought.

"You wanted to see me, boss?" Johnny Ray stopped next to the small cart that contained a coffeemaker and disposable cups—a show of hospitality when government officials visited Mr. Broad.

"Find the King of L.A. and have him check out those unfamiliars." He pointed to the tele-skin.

Johnny Ray surveyed the screen and clicked his tongue. "Cyberpunks?"

"Must be. I can't see any implants in that area on the map."

"Banded together. Is that the subway? So predictable," Johnny Ray scoffed. "It's laughable that they think they have any margin of success."

Mr. Broad, stature matching his surname, straightened his posture to expose his full six-foot-seven height. Johnny Ray, not short by any means, now appeared like a dwarf next to Mr. Broad. Calmly and without emotion, he said, "The moment we underestimate those with only passion and a motivation to wake them up in the morning is the moment everything I've worked for crumbles into their hands. And I won't allow miscalculations to be the downfall of my empire."

Johnny Ray held his breath for a beat. Mr. Broad's behavior over the years had taught Johnny Ray one thing: the calmer Mr. Broad became, the more severe threats became. Johnny Ray nodded in understanding, afraid to give a verbal answer for his voice might crack in fear. That would bode even worse for Cyber-Corp's number two in charge.

"Grab the King of L.A. and snuff out that rogue band. I don't know how they got so close to Factory Medusa undetected, but that's too close for comfort."

"Yes, sir. They will be gone by morning."

Mr. Broad whipped his head toward his assistant and growled, "They will be gone *tonight*."

011000011111000111011100

Johnny Ray strode through the empty cubicles of Cyber-Corp as he spoke aloud. "Lancelot?"

"Yes, sir." The robotic voice seemed to not just come from the walls and the ceiling but from the very essence of the building itself.

"Send a message to the King of L.A. He's to meet me at the corner of—" He clipped the corner of a desk as he turned a corner and swore under his breath, rubbing his thigh.

"Sir? Corner of where?"

"McCarty and Medders."

"Roger that, sir."

Johnny Ray used his palm to push through the glass doors that led from the office area and into the small living quarters of Cyber-Corp's employees. He strode past orange wooden door after orange wooden door of studio apartments, whose occupants were hopefully asleep and ready to wake up bright-eyed and bushy-tailed for another day of doing the good deeds that the status quo population didn't know they needed, all to maintain their blissful lifestyles.

Johnny Ray's orange penny loafers padded on the orange carpet as he maintained his pace toward the stairwell.

"Sir, I could not locate the King of L.A.," Lancelot said, the mechanical voice filling the hallway.

"I know where he might be," Johnny Ray grumbled. "Thank you anyway, Lancelot."

The computer didn't respond.

Johnny Ray descended the stairwell, as if his legs were windmills, toward the ground floor. Stairs, landing, and turn. Stairs, landing, and turn. Stairs … When he hit the bottom, he pushed through Cyber-Corp's main doors that led into the downtown area. The wind whipped his orange trench coat, and he pushed down the sidewalk toward where he would find the King of L.A. on any given night when he *wasn't* answering Lancelot's calls.

The orange skyscrapers surrounding the city streets boxed in the residents, sprawling skyward almost as far as the eye could see. All inhabited by sleeping citizens, their Synchestria Implants recording their dreams—or what they saw and heard if one were to sleepwalk or to get up in the middle of the night for whatever reason—so Cyber-Corp could upload that information into the Net and use it to make their lives a better existence. It infuriated Johnny Ray to think how some citizens didn't realize Cyber-Corp's existence was to make a better tomorrow for these people.

And then there were the cyberpunks—the epitome of an enemy, trying to eradicate the one megacorporation who was making a positive difference in the world. Johnny Ray's stomach boiled whenever he thought of those spoiled brats. Knowing one day that he would personally be responsible for their undoing was what made him forgo sleep, forgo relationships, forgo any semblance of a life.

Johnny Ray ran a hand through his thinning hair and entered the lot reserved for Cyber-Corp superiors. He strode toward the tall rectangular box and stepped inside. He closed the door, and the darkness consumed him for a moment, until bright orange LED lights illuminated the small space, like a stand-up coffin. A finger scanner flashed orange, and Johnny Ray placed his thumb on the screen.

"What's your destination?" asked a voice that sounded like Lancelot, though it was not tied into Lancelot's mainframe.

"Peppermint Lounge," Johnny Ray answered.

A single flash of blinding orange light filled the box, and Johnny Ray was no longer standing there. The door to the Brundle Teleporter opened automatically to reveal its vacant space, waiting for its next prepaid passenger.

4

Cain lifted his orange grime-covered goggles and removed his orange leather mask from his face. He tilted his head and beheld the woman on his table. Her eyes still open, motionless—*lifeless* was more accurate. Cain hoped she had finally found paradise in Shangri-la and that she was free from the monstrosities of this world.

The neuro-trancer set the empty syringe onto the tray next to the heart monitor that now issued a single steady tone. It wasn't her lifeless eyes staring ceilingward that made him uncomfortable—especially after the many trancing sessions Cain had performed on those who wanted to be free—but how her arm dangled off the table and hung suspended. He grabbed her wrist and delicately placed her arm onto her chest, then clicked off the heart monitor. The room fell into silence.

A knock sounded on the only door to the room, and Cain sputtered through a croaky voice, "Come in."

The door swung open, and a woman—with similar grime-covered goggles hanging around her neck—entered the operating theatre. "How'd it go?"

Cain pursed his lips and lovingly eyed the female on the table. "She's with Mother Dawn now."

"Praise Mother Dawn."

Cain mumbled the appropriate response, "Mother Dawn be praised."

"I have another trancing session in about an hour," Clawdy said, approaching him. "So, if you can wait, we can dispose of the bodies together."

Cain grabbed the back of Clawdy's neck and pulled her in for a kiss, his lips pressed firmly against her dusty ones, their goggles around their necks clacking against each other. "That sounds fine," he said, after pulling away. "Who's your trancing session today?"

Clawdy moved toward the cabinet filled with syringes and trancing fluids. She opened the door and collected the supplies she would need for her patient. "Male. In his late thirties."

Cain nodded once. "Trying to get to Shangri-la before he expires."

"Probably." Clawdy turned to face Cain, the needles and vials of fluid secure in the crook of her arm. "Have you ever thought about when it'll be time for us? You know, to go to Shangri-la?"

Cain shifted his weight and scratched the back of his neck. "We took an oath as neuro-trancers, to stay here as long as possible, to help the people find true salvation. Our time comes when we are two breaths from our final one. No sooner."

A shroud of disappointment fell upon Clawdy. "I knew you would say that. Can't help but sometimes be jealous of all these people we set free."

"We're doing Mother Dawn's work."

"Praise Mother Dawn," Clawdy mumbled unenthusiastically.

"Mother Dawn be praised. Now set up your room for the trancing."

Clawdy offered an *mmm-hmm* without opening her mouth and turned for the door.

"My sweet?" Cain said, stopping her. "I love you."

Clawdy did not turn to face him when she answered, "Love you too." Then she exited the trancing room, heading for her own.

011000011111000111011100

"Do you want to be hypnotized?" Clawdy asked the man—customer, client, patient? She still didn't know how to appropriately refer to them.

This question was number one on the neuro-trancers' rules of trancing. The neuro-trancer must ask the customer/client/patient this question *before* they can begin the trancing. Without getting at least a verbal affirmation from the subject, Mother Dawn would not allow the customer to taste salvation in the afterlife.

"I do," the man said and swiveled his body onto the table without any prompting from Clawdy.

The problem was, Clawdy had started doubting the existence of this Mother Dawn deity some time ago. She slept better on those nights when she admitted to herself that she remained a neuro-trancer not for Mother Dawn but for doing the right thing for the people who wanted to reach paradise before death.

"Do you have any questions?" She raised her grime-covered goggles dangling around her neck and covered her eyes.

"No, ma'am. I've been ready for this for a long, long time." He settled his back and head into a comfortable position and closed his eyes.

"One last piece of business." She tapped his arm so he would open his eyes and handed him a keypad. "You must donate all your credits to Mother Dawn, as payment for entrance into her paradise."

The man entered his identification number, transferring his life savings into the neuro-trancer account, and closed his eyes again.

Clawdy filled a syringe with the orange trancing fluid and turned on the heart monitor. She grabbed his bare forearm and pushed the needle into his vein.

"Praise Mother Dawn," the man said. Then he went lifeless.

Clawdy swallowed hard and sighed. "Mother Dawn be praised," she replied, barely in a whisper. She placed both palms on her nearby desk that stored her journals and closed her eyes. She inhaled deeply, held it, and blew it out slowly, trying to find her true north inside her soul. Failing that, she opened her eyes.

An engulfing feeling of loneliness and claustrophobia filled her. She felt as if the walls were closing in. She wondered if what she and her brethren were doing here in the commune was all a lie. Her doubts and negative emotion wouldn't stop, not until they smothered her.

Or until she went mad, if she didn't find an answer to her purpose soon.

5

Adam lay in his cot, Venus cuddled under his arm and her head on his chest. He listened to her sleepy shallow breathing while he stared ceilingward, thinking how fortunate he had been to find this band of misfits. How lucky he had been to find Venus.

Thoughts of penetrating one of Cyber-Corp's factories played out in his mind like moving images—or what the ancients had called *movies*. He guessed that word made sense. Not everything the ancients had done was that idiotic, as history class in school had wanted them to believe. Sure, the ancients were primitive creatures, still using crude vehicles as a form of transportation—instead of the Brundle Teleporters—but technology hadn't caught up to them yet.

Adam shuddered; he couldn't imagine living in such a primordial environment. He thanked Mother Dawn that he had been born during the Age of Oblivion—as the megacorporations had titled the current era of the world. Not the Age of Destruction—again what Cyber-Corp had deemed the time in history before they had invented the Synchestria Implants.

Still Adam wondered if his passion for learning about the ancients really meant that maybe he had been meant for *that* time instead. It also irked him how the megacorporations had the self-appointed power to name certain eras of the earth's history and to add those so-called facts into the school system.

That irrational thought-rabbit hole reminded Adam why he had gone rogue and had sought the cyberpunk cells in the first place. He had heard about governments, when they were behemoths during the Age of Destruction, not the sniveling cowards they had become under the megacorporations' rule.

Adam thought those must have been glorious times to be alive. And the cyberpunks would see to it that they restored power to those who had the citizens' best intentions at heart—not using them for data-collecting and to perfect artificial intelligence technology.

Venus shifted her body against him and wiped her nose without opening her eyes or waking up.

Adam lifted his head so his lips could reach the crown of her head, where he planted a delicate kiss. He knew he should sleep; tomorrow would be detrimental to the megacorporations' cause but also dangerous enough to Adam's band where some of them, if not all, could be killed during the raid.

That was the unspoken vow that every cyberpunk took when they either refused their Synchestria Implant or, in some extreme cases, had a 3-11 Man remove implants before going underground. Adam thought those were the real badasses. It was one thing to deny Cyber-Corp to install their implant; it was another thing entirely to find a 3-11 Man in some dirty garage or back alley to have him remove the implant. Adam couldn't imagine the courage it took to let some makeshift surgeon mess around too near to his brain.

But regardless of *how* someone joined the cyberpunk movement, the important thing was that they were all in it together—his band of deviants plus all the countless cells of others he had heard about, springing up all over the different provinces. If they could take down just this one factory, it might be a small blip in the overall war, but Adam would sleep at night—or die peacefully, if tomorrow comes to that—knowing his troops had aided the cause.

Venus scratched her nose in her sleep again, but this time her eyelids fluttered open. She haphazardly propped herself on an elbow. "Can't sleep?"

His ice-blue eyes found her face, and his heart blipped. He didn't answer right away, wanting to behold her first. Most people didn't find their partner until they were in their thirties, which only gave them ten or so years to produce offspring before they died.

He marveled at the Age of Destruction's people—the *ancients*—who lived to almost one hundred years old. Adam fantasized frequently about what it would be like to live in an era when children knew their parents, where their parents actually raised them, not shucked onto the streets to fend for themselves, usually as a preteen, because that was the age of children when most of their parents would die.

Adam's silence prompted Venus to speak again. "What'chya thinking about?" She used her fingernail to trace the exposed skin of his bicep.

Adan wiggled himself into a seated position. "Ever wonder what it would be like to have a family as an adult?"

Venus sighed and duplicated his posture. "Thinking about the ancients again. Always with your head in the past."

"Ya know, if you weren't so completely adorable, I would have stopped putting up with you a long time ago."

"Oh, yeah? Then why do you still put up with Jonesy? I don't think *adorable* would ever be used to describe him." She winked and bit her bottom lip.

Adam chuckled and playfully punched her shoulder. "I don't ever doubt that we are doing the right thing, but sometimes I wonder if it's all moot in the end anyway. Because … you know."

"Because the life expectancy is getting shorter and shorter. Would you really *want* to live to seventy or eighty or even, ugh, ninety? That sounds terrible."

Adam picked at his cuticle and thought hard. "Does it ever bother you how Cyber-Corp doesn't even have guards protecting their buildings and factories?"

"That would create public mistrust," she murmured. "Cyber-Corp is all about creating an illusion that they are doing good for the people. It's all perception. Now shut up and hold me."

Adam smirked and slithered into a prone position and grabbed her tightly.

"And stop worrying about silly things," Venus added, then resumed her shallow breathing. Asleep once again.

Adam closed his eyes and hoped sleep was just around the corner for him too, but he couldn't shake a nagging feeling. As he drifted off to sleep, his last thought was that he hoped all six of his band would still be alive and together come this time tomorrow.

6

The Brundle Teleporter located farther inside the city flashed with orange LED lights. Johnny Ray shook his head to clear the cobwebs from his brain that always came with teleporting, then opened the coffinlike door. This was the closest teleporter to the Peppermint Lounge, but he welcomed the four-block walk to reach the pub.

His orange penny loafers moved down the sidewalk—the width of what the ancients had called *streets* during the Age of Destruction—toward the flashing marquee that announced the lounge's name in glorious orange lettering. Johnny Ray reached the doors lickety-split; he couldn't understand why anyone would want to move at a snail's pace, not when life was so short and there was so much to accomplish.

He pushed through the wooden double doors to reveal scattered round tables, each with a different number of chairs, and homed in on the bar counter at the far end of the lounge. He strode toward the sole gentleman facing the barkeep, his back to Johnny Ray.

The barkeep noticed Johnny Ray first and donned a fake grin in greeting. This tipped off the man whose back was to Johnny Ray that someone was approaching, and he turned at the waist. Johnny Ray noticed how the King of L.A.'s body slumped in a sarcastic *oh great* movement, before the man refocused on the barkeep and faced his backside to Johnny Ray once more.

Johnny Ray slipped onto the stool next to the King of L.A. and placed both elbows on the bar counter.

"What's your poison?" the barkeep asked.

"Just here to talk to my friend," Johnny Ray said.

"No drink. No talk." The barkeep stepped backward and folded his arms.

"Fine. Give me a whatever." Johnny Ray faced the King of L.A. as the barkeep turned to make some concoction. "Mr. Broad wants you."

The King of L.A. vigorously rubbed his white beard with his palm. The strands of coarse hair audibly scratching against the man's leathery skin. "I know. Lancelot tried calling me. I ignored the signal."

Johnny Ray took a deep breath to steel himself against saying something he might regret later. Cyber-Corp needed this man. Well, they needed *all* assassins, but the King of L.A. was special. Johnny Ray contemplated his next statement while admiring—something he would never ever admit to—the man sitting next to him.

The King of L.A. was a force to be reckoned with. His stature and commanding presence affected any room he entered. The long scar that traveled from his forehead, down across a permanently shut eyelid hid an empty eye socket, and ended at his chin could tell stories that would make even the most-hardened assassins quiver. His white beard matched the color of his full head of curly hair.

Johnny Ray suspected that the King of L.A. had done *something* in his past—a deal with the devil maybe—that had allowed him to age well-beyond the normal life expectancy. Rumors were the King of L.A. was in his sixties. While this seemed unfathomable to Johnny Ray, he had no other explanation for the man's white hair, wrinkled face, and a history of war stories that went back decades upon decades.

"Mr. Broad doesn't like it when people don't answer," Johnny Ray finally said.

"I don't work for him." The King of L.A. swiveled to glare at Johnny Ray. "You pipsqueaks do. I work for myself, which is why he sent *you* to locate *me*."

"You make it easy to find you. Seems that would be detrimental for an assassin."

The King of L.A. squinted his one good eye at Johnny Ray. He raised his glass to his lips and paused. "Your drink is ready."

Johnny Ray glanced at the bar counter and saw the barkeep had left him a mixture of something bubbly. He then faced the King of L.A. "We have a cell of cyberpunks that Mr. Broad wants you to take care of. Tonight. Underground. Subway tunnels. Drone spotted them."

The King of L.A. cleared his throat and raised an eyebrow. "I said, your drink is ready."

Johnny Ray let his shoulders relax, defeated. "Fine. Whatever." He brought the glass to his lips and took a swig. He craned his chin forward to help the liquid slide down his throat. "Now will you talk to me?"

The King of L.A. laughed and clapped his hands one time. "Man, you are a trip." He gripped Johnny Ray's shoulder and shook it, as if they were best buds. "Yeah, yeah. I got nothing to do tonight."

"The drone was scouting platform 10-19-94."

"How many?"

"Six silhouettes."

"Easy day," the King of L.A. replied and took another sip. "Is this *capture and bring before His Highness*, or is this *make them go away?*"

Johnny Ray leaned in closer. "Only cyberpunks stay like rats in the tunnels. And they are really close to Factory Medusa."

The King of L.A. raised one eyebrow. "Oh? Can't let anything happen to Cyber-Corp's main building and corporate suites, now can we?" He chuckled, then brought his glass to his mouth again.

"I will assume that you'll exterminate this infestation before sunrise?" Johnny Ray patted the King of L.A.'s thigh to drive home his point.

"And I assume the appropriate funds will be transferred to my account before sunset?"

"Nothing has changed with our contract. And Mr. Broad has reinstated your thumbprint so you can use the Brundles."

"Good," the King of L.A. said and swiped Johnny Ray's hand off his thigh. "Then we are done talking. Finish your drink and scurry away."

7

A knock on the door brought Clawdy from her trance. "Come in," she called out.

The door opened to reveal Cain. "How'd it go?" He glanced at the man on the table.

"One of the easier ones. Had no reservations." She tried to shake out the feelings she had been struggling with a few moments before so Cain wouldn't suspect that she was having anything but the purest of thoughts.

"Good. Good." Cain entered the room and stopped at the foot of the table. "Let's dispose of the bodies and go get something to eat." He stripped his goggles up and over his head and laid them on a counter, then left the room to get the cadaver boxes.

Clawdy closed her eyes, swimming in her recurring fantasy that a wonderland existed beyond the borders of the commune, yet a short-lived fantasy because Cain would return soon, and they had to get to work.

Cain cleared his throat to get her attention. She opened her eyes to see him approaching her. With one eye squinted in suspicion, he said, "You were swaying."

Clawdy ran a fingernail through an eyebrow. "So? Tiring day. Let's get the bodies out of here."

Unwavered, Cain leaned in closer. "You're having those thoughts again."

Clawdy placed her face in her hands and spoke through the slits in her fingers. "It's getting harder." She let a small squeak of a sob escape to help express her feelings, hoping he would go easy on her.

Cain grabbed her wrists and pulled her hands from her face. "Listen. We have a greater paradise waiting for us when it's our time. Mother Dawn promises us. However, she looks down on us when we have urges of curiosity or doubt. You know that. *Thy will not yearn for any paradise other than the one I have created for my children in Shangri-la.* Her words."

Clawdy stepped backward and balled her fists, angry that he never could entertain a few *what-if* theories and always held steadfast to his dogma. "And how do we know she said that? Who heard her say that? And when? We've just blindly been indoctrinated into believing Mother Dawn."

Cain raised his hand in a *stop* motion. "Do you need to leave the commune? If you are questioning your faith, then you cannot be a neuro-trancer."

Clawdy studied his face—a face she had fallen in love with years ago, so soft and kind and wise. But not now. Now it projected confusion and disappointment. Disappointment in her. And she didn't think she could exist if Cain was disappointed in her.

So … she dug deep and let the words flow from her mouth that she did not believe in, just so he would stay with her. Just so she could remain in the commune and around Cain. "Praise Mother Dawn."

"Mother Dawn be praised." Cain's smile reached from ear to ear. "Feel better?"

She forced a nod but did not reply. Could not reply. Her head was throbbing.

"All right, let's box up these people and head to dinner."

"Sounds good," she mumbled.

"And, Clawdy?"

Her gaze met his.

"No more faltering. Promise?"

She nodded and crossed her fingers inside her mind—for she had heard that was what the ancients had done, if they were to lie to someone.

011000011111000111011100

Cain swung open the wooden door to the communal area, and he and Clawdy hung their goggles on the rows of hooks that had different-sized eyewear dangling from them.

"Wonder where everyone is," Cain mused and headed toward the dining hall.

Clawdy followed and saw that the rest of the neuro-trancers were already seated at tables and eating.

"Long day trancing?" one of them asked as Cain and Clawdy entered the dining hall.

"Clawdy had a late appointment," Cain answered. "Smells good. Any left?"

They wove through the tables of neuro-trancers and reached the food counter.

"Saved these plates for you," the cook said and placed two trays on the counter.

"Much obliged." Cain grabbed both trays and headed toward an empty table.

Clawdy followed and sat across from him, defeated, yet forcing herself to resume her mundane guise.

"You got any appointments tomorrow?" he asked while shoveling food into his mouth.

"Nah. Tomorrow is free."

"I only have an early morning trancing session. You wanna go to the temple in the afternoon?"

Clawdy sighed louder than she had intended. Whenever she could get out of going to the temple, she would. She felt nothing was more of a waste of time than spending hours in silence, praying to Mother Dawn, in a large stone structure. They were doing *her* work as neuro-trancers; shouldn't that be enough for her? Why do they also have to spend their free time praying? It felt so primitive to Clawdy.

"I would love to," she replied—but wished she could let him know that the *love to* part was directed at spending time with Cain and didn't have anything to do with Mother Dawn.

The occupants of one of the tables all stood together and dropped their empty trays onto the counter near the kitchen. One tall, lanky man approached their table, his few-days-old stubble showing signs of gray.

He'll be dead soon, Clawdy thought.

He smacked his lips and said, "We're gonna go trip the light fantastic. You guys want in?"

Cain glared at Clawdy, silently scolding her to not say anything but a negative response.

Clawdy looked down and answered for them both. "No thanks. We're good tonight."

The man nodded and walked away from the table to catch up with the other neuro-trancers who were headed to the field to play music and to dance through the night.

Clawdy conjured some courage to say, "Why do you care so much if I want to have some fun and dance? Can you show me anywhere in Mother Dawn's teachings where she says *anything* about music and dance being forbidden or sacrilege? You can't. Plus you don't have any issues with them doing it."

Cain used his fingernail to pick at a piece of lodged food. "Because I am not mated with any of them."

Clawdy used every ounce of willpower to squash the rising anger inside her. "And all you see of me is someone to procreate with?"

Cain lowered his head and glared at her through the bottom of his eyebrows. "Mother Dawn blessed us with life so we can create more life for her. And I chose you and only you for that sacred mission. You should be honored."

Clawdy let her fork drop from her grasp and *clank* on the plate. Then she sat back in her chair and folded her arms. "And what about romance? And passion? Does it always have to be about just procreation with you?"

Cain scooped another forkful of food into his mouth and answered around the chewed bits in his mouth, "That's the thinking of the ancients. Their civilization fell because they put too much weight on this idealistic belief in love. The only love that exists in the world is the love that Mother Dawn has for her children. And our job is to create more beings for her to love. In fact"—he waggled his fork at her—"you could even say that, if we love one another, then we are being blasphemous. Love is reserved for her and for her only."

Clawdy pushed out her chair and stood.

"Where are you going?" he asked, his eyebrows furrowed.

"Gonna go dance with people who actually understand what it means to live. Mother Dawn or not."

Cain's face remained stoic, but she thought she saw a flash of panic cross it. He calmly and without emotion said, "Have fun. I won't wait up for you."

Clawdy slid the chair under the table and double stepped out the dining hall to catch up with her fellow neuro-trancers, leaving Cain to eat in solitude.

01100001 11110001 11011100

Clawdy saw the group of neuro-trancers turn the corner around one of the commune buildings and called out, "Hey, guys! Wait up."

The man in the rear of the pack, holding a circular drum covered with animal hide, stopped and turned. His smile lit up his face as soon as he saw her. "Didn't think you were coming," Judas said.

Clawdy trotted toward him. "Cain didn't want me to come."

"And what made you change your mind?"

They walked side by side now, following the group into the field.

Clawdy debated not answering at all or maybe lying. It was well known throughout the commune that she and Cain were an item, but what did that even mean if she yearned for love and passion, and all he saw was her fertile womb?

"Cain answered for me."

Judas walked in silence but nodded in understanding.

Clawdy put her hand on his arm to stop him. "Do you think Mother Dawn doesn't want us to love each other?"

Judas put a knuckle to his lips and sighed. "I think the only thing Mother Dawn wants us to do is love each other."

Clawdy shook her head. "No, I don't mean care about each other. I mean love each other. Romantically."

"Well, I'll be honest, Clawdy. That opens a whole Pandora's Box of issues, as the ancients would have said. It's better to not let romantic love cloud our mission. I don't agree with some of Cain's extremist beliefs about Mother Dawn, but I do think romantic love can hinder procreation, especially when we are only on this Earth for such a short amount of time."

They started walking again and met up with the rest of the group, who were sitting in the field, passing around small trinkets of noisemakers and percussion instruments. Clawdy and Judas sat cross-legged, facing each other, on the outskirts of the group, as the rhythmic music started.

Clawdy closed her eyes and swayed to the beat, and her heart rate increased, anticipating the euphoria that ecstatic dance would bring once she fell in step to the rhythm. She tucked a strand of her brown hair behind her ear and looked into Judas's orange eyes. "He claims he can hear her."

Judas paused and turned his face slightly to the side. "Come again?"

Clawdy released a long exhale. She had never spoken those words aloud.

Cain had forbidden her to say anything to anyone; he claimed they would either banish him from the commune for being delusional or would revere him as a saint—something he said would be blasphemous against their female deity.

"Cain says he can hear Mother Dawn. She talks directly to him."

Judas chortled and shook his head. "Like, words?"

"*Uh-huh.* He says she communicates with him in his sleep. And she sounds like layers of static, with each layer having a different tone. Then the layers morph into a single note."

"I see …" Judas's eyes widened in sarcasm. "Sounds like he's already halfway to his own personal Shangri-la."

"I don't think he's crazy. He says it with such conviction."

"Most crazies do," Judas said, rising to proffer a hand for her to stand and to meet his height. "Now, ssshhhh. Let's just enjoy the ride."

Clawdy turned her back to Judas, raised her arms above her head, let her hands relax, and moved her hips with the orchestrated drumming coming from her fellow neuro-trancers. Euphoria shot through every ounce of her being as thoughts of Cain claiming that Mother Dawn talked to him in tones broke apart like puzzle pieces and spiraled away from her.

S

The King of L.A. used his pinkie to slide some stubborn food from between two teeth as he surveyed the stairs that descended into the subway. Platform 10-19-94 was what Johnny Ray had told him. Six cyberpunks. Should be an easy payday; he'll soon report to Mr. Broad that he had taken care of the marks, meanwhile adding more freedom fighters to the cause.

The King of L.A. shuffled down the stairs leading underground, the orange LEDs from above fading into darkness the farther he descended. He stopped when the illumination above was completely gone so his eyes could adjust to the lack of light. Outlines emerged in his vision, allowing him to map his trajectory in front of him now.

Stealthily and silently, he reached the bottom of the stairs and hurdled over the turnstile—such an archaic device used by the ancients in a primitive time. His feet made a clopping sound when they landed on the other side, and he noticed the sound did not echo back to him. The depths of this tunnel must be endless.

The King of L.A. scratched his white beard, his one good eye scanning the darkness for any movement. So far, so good. Didn't want to spook them too far away from his approach. He moved against the wall to use it as a guide farther into the tunnel, the railway tracks to his right. His experience over the years from recruiting cyberpunks told him that they were probably using the subway offices as their bedrooms.

His good eye spotted a low smoldering fire, possibly a recently extinguished firepit, and smelled the leftover rodent stew. He smiled in the darkness. This cell was resourceful. They would make a terrific addition to the movement. Get the kids to safety and tell Cyber-Corp that he had eliminated them, then collect payment in full. It wasn't an all-out lie.

Mr. Broad just wanted the assassins to deal with the cyberpunks and have them out of Cyber-Corp's hair. The King of L.A. did just that. Except recruiting them for the war against the megacorporations probably wasn't what Mr. Broad had in mind every time he hired the King of L.A. to dispose of these cyberpunk cells.

His fingers tap-danced along the wall, feeling for a corner or a hallway, as he maintained his trajectory toward the offices. Toward the sleeping teens. He cracked his jaw to relieve some pressure before he revealed himself. This was always the most dangerous part—how to look like an assassin on the outside but try to convince these cells that he was fighting on their side, all within a split second before they panicked and reacted.

The offices of platform 10-19-94 came into his view, and he unholstered his clipper and powered it on, the firearm glowing orange that signaled it was activated, in case the teens had posted a trigger-happy lookout, and he needed it for self-defense.

He squinted his good eye to focus better on the offices ahead. He discerned two lumps through the window of the first office, huddled close together.

His orange boots landed softly, one after the other. He opened the door slowly and planned to close it behind him, then make his presence known, identifying himself as friend. He found when people were roused abruptly from slumber, their reaction times were slower, giving him a few extra ticks to explain who he was and why he was there—but footsteps shuffling outside the office caught his attention.

He ducked and found concealment behind a desk. Dammit, he thought, someone was awake and wandering around—probably their lookout. Staying in a crouched position, the King of L.A. scooted out the open office door, leaving the young man and female sleeping on the cot, and slunk onto the subway platform. He spotted the wanderer stop about twenty yards ahead and squat against the wall to urinate.

He crouched closer and noticed the girl had her face in her hands as she relieved herself. "*Psst*," he whispered, then glanced behind him to ensure he didn't wake the ones who were sleeping nearby. This was when it was most dangerous. Cyberpunks would die for their cause, so he didn't want to startle anyone but, at the same time, had to reveal his true intentions.

"*Psst!*" Louder this time—the sound reverberating down the tunnel.

Still nothing.

The King of L.A. inched closer to the girl, his clipper gripped in his hands for a *just in case*, and said louder, "Hey … I'm here to help you."

The woman didn't flinch. Didn't take her face from her hands. Didn't look up at him.

No way she didn't hear him. The subway was dense with silence. Any sound, no matter how minuscule, was like thunder down here. He cleared his throat loudly.

And still nothing.

The girl was obviously finished doing her business because she stood, turned away from the King of L.A., and pulled up her pants.

In his decades of reconnaissance, he had never felt so perplexed—or so *ignored*.

But that all changed when the woman turned to head back to her office bedroom and saw him and his weapon. Then she screamed and raised an old-timey pistol.

The King of L.A.'s good eye widened at the sight of the barrel aimed for his face, and he instinctively let out three rounds at the girl's body. The plasma bolts from his clipper found their mark in the screaming girl, neutralizing the threat. One, two, three. Stomach, chest, forehead. She fell backward, lifeless, on the subway platform.

He was now living the worst-case scenario.

0110000111110001110111100

The sound of someone screaming startled Adam awake. Jumping to his feet also rose Venus. Adrenaline coursed through his body as Adam sprinted for the office door. He had never heard Maggie scream like that before. In fact, he hadn't heard Maggie say anything before, but he knew in his gut that their deaf friend had screamed. The sound of her voice sent shivers up his spine.

Venus pushed past him when he reached the doorway. "That's Maggie!"

"I know," he said and let Venus go through first.

He watched Venus run across the platform toward Maggie's body on the ground and stopped to acclimate his eyes to the situation. He spotted the orange glow of a clipper farther down the platform. He could barely decipher a human standing close to the train tracks, their weapon helping to expose their position.

So Adam ran.

He ran with everything his muscles could handle.

As he ran straight for the man, he stole a glimpse across the platform of Maggie sprawled on the platform, motionless. Possibly dead.

That was when he dug his heels into the pavement and drew closer to the man, hearing him saying something. The heartbeat thumping in Adam's ears had become so loud that it muffled anybody's voice—even the monster's whose mouth was saying *something*. Adam launched himself at the intruder.

0110000011110001110111100

The King of L.A. froze when he saw the ice-blue eyes of the boy atop him. Those eyes rendered him motionless. Those eyes, blue among generations of orange ones.

He had found the missing link. He had found the liberator. The savior.

Then the boy's fist smashed into his face, and blackness consumed him.

0110000011110001110111100

Rage engulfed Adam as he brought his fist behind his head and shot it forward to pummel the man he had tackled.

Panting and dizzy, Adam stopped smashing his fist into the man's face and stumble-ran to where he saw Venus kneeling over Maggie's body.

"What the hell is going on?" Jonesy yelled from across the platform, exiting his office.

"Get everyone up!" Adam commanded and slid on his knees when he reached the two girls. Adam leaned across to their fallen friend.

Maggie's eyes were open, staring lifelessly, and blood soaked her shirt. Crimson covered half her face from the hole in her forehead.

Adam snorted quick breaths through his nose like a bull, ready to return to the man on the floor to smash in more of his face.

Adam knew Venus had realized the fate of their comrade when Venus wailed, the sounds of her grief traveling down the subway tunnel but not echoing back to them, like the darkness was eating her sadness. Adam spotted Cherie running from her office toward Venus's cries but noticed Mony heading toward the man on the ground.

Adam rose and met Mony at the unconscious intruder.

"What do you think? A junkie chasing the dragon too many times? All doped up?" Mony asked without any emotion.

"I don't think so." Adam lowered himself for a better look. "He looks … old."

"Yeah, well, he killed Maggie, so we should tie him up and wait for him to come to."

Adam growled. Immediate guilt consumed him for not acknowledging Maggie's state. "Stay here and watch him. If he starts to wake up, kick him in the teeth."

"With pleasure," Mony said.

Adam sprinted across the platform toward the rest of his crew, who were expressing a mixture of sobs and cries as they kneeled around Maggie. He stopped behind Jonesy and beheld Maggie's lifeless form.

Cherie looked up at him with a snarl. "What are we gonna do to that piece of shit? And, if I don't agree, I'm gonna do what *I* want to him."

"I told Mony that she could kick in his teeth if he wakes. I want to tie him up and get him into my office."

Venus took her gaze off Maggie's body and met Adam's. "Do you think he's just a junkie, or were we targeted?"

"I dunno, but I'm gonna find out. Someone get a blanket to cover Maggie." Adam strutted toward his office, glancing at Mony to ensure she was focused on the man who had killed Maggie. Adam felt a smirk tug at the corner of his lips when he saw that Mony had a boot half raised over the man's face. Maybe they should just rip him apart.

"Hey, Mony," he yelled as he continued toward his office.

She looked up at him.

"His weapon is right there on the platform. Grab it and maybe shoot him in his legs and arms when he wakes up."

In the darkness, Adam thought he saw Mony smirk. He got inside his office, grabbed the spool of wire that an ancient had left here so many eons ago, and headed back for the man.

Adam noticed that Mony had the clipper tucked into the front of her waistband, and he nodded in approval. He offered the spool of wire to her, and she held it while he unraveled enough to wrap the man's arms and legs. Then Adam took a knife from his pocket and cut the wire. Mony tossed the spool onto the platform with a clatter, and, before Adam wrapped the man in the wire, he glanced toward the rest of his crew. They now stood around Maggie's fallen body. Adam would deal with his grief later. Right now, he needed to secure this possible junkie and get him into the office.

"Come on. Give me a hand."

Mony lifted the man's body off the platform so Adam could wind the wire around the man's torso, including his arms. Around and around, he spun the wire. When he felt confident that he had secured the man, he slipped the knife into his pocket and manipulated the man into a sitting position.

The man opened his one good eye, and Mony brought her boot backward to kick out his teeth. And hopefully kick in his skull.

9

"Do you want to be hypnotized?" Cain asked the man on the table, his gusto and enthusiasm now waned. He couldn't rip from his mind the thoughts of Clawdy going off to dance and to frolic with the others yesterday. And now it was affecting his job. His meaning for existing. His full focus to do Mother Dawn's bidding.

And that was not okay.

"Yes ... yes, I do. But ..." the man stammered.

Patience ran thin in Cain as he snapped, "But, what?"

"How do we know Shangri-la is on the other side of the trancing? What if it's just ... death?"

Cain secured the orange leather mask over his face and adjusted the grime-covered goggles over his eyes. The mask now muffled his voice. "Praise Mother Dawn."

The man, sitting upright on the table, glared at Cain. "That's it? That's all you're going to say? It can't be that simple."

Cain turned on the heart monitor and grabbed a needle from the tray. "Mother Dawn makes it that simple. And she's offended that you spoke before giving the appropriate response."

The man furrowed his brows. "What are you talking about?"

In a flash, Cain spun and grabbed the man's throat. "I said, Praise Mother Dawn. She expects you to reply with"—he squeezed harder—"Mother Dawn be praised."

The man's eyes widened, and he swatted Cain's hand off his throat. "You are a lunatic. No way I'm gonna let you put me under." He scooted off the table and pushed through the closed door and into the hallway.

Cain ran the syringe through his fingers, admiring the orange liquid inside. The liquid that held Shangri-la. The liquid that held the lifeforce of Mother Dawn herself. It was fine if some became nonbelievers. She just would not welcome them into her paradise. Cain knew it was not his job to convert anyone. Mother Dawn had made it clear in her layers of tone when she had spoken to him that his vocation was to assist her children into the Promised Land.

Clawdy appeared in the open doorway. "What happened? You okay?"

Her voice broke him from his thoughts, and he forced a smile. "Yeah, yeah. I'm fine. Guy got cold feet. Last-minute jitters. You know how it is."

She nodded and approached him and rubbed his arms. "You're not mad about yesterday, right? I just needed to let off some steam."

Cain slid his goggles off his eyes and set them on his forehead.

Clawdy pulled his leather mask from his mouth and set it on the tray of needles.

"Not mad at all. I love that you keep me on my toes." He wrapped his arms around her and brought her in for a hug.

She closed her eyes and smiled, just feeling his strength and warmth and love. Even if he believed Mother Dawn didn't permit romantic love, she pretended in these moments that he loved her in that way regardless.

011000011111000111011100

Clawdy held her breath when they entered their commune barracks room. Cain had stormed through the door and flung his goggles on his bed. It wasn't that she necessarily disliked it when he was angry. It was more that he became so unpredictable. And, within these moments, she questioned why she loved him at all.

Clawdy exhaled slowly to not make a noise and infuriate him further. If he kept his aggression targeted on inanimate objects, his fist would avoid her face. Not always but sometimes.

Cain took a deep breath and held it; Clawdy focused on how raised and tense his shoulders looked. He spun on his heels and pointed at her chest. "Why do they taunt me?"

She swallowed hard and contemplated her answer with surgical precision. She could ask who he meant, or she could give him an answer, not knowing who he meant. Her silence must have gone on too long for him because he spoke again, unprompted.

"Why would they book a trancing appointment, travel all the way out here, waste *my* time, just to leave when they're on the table?" Cain paced like a caged animal, not making eye contact with Clawdy.

She was not entirely convinced that he was even talking *to* her right now. He might just need to vent—to her, to the floor, to maybe Mother Dawn herself.

"Nonbelievers will be the downfall of our utopia to the paradise Mother Dawn has promised us." He stopped pacing and met her gaze, *Now* he was talking to Clawdy—his glare palpable. "Too many uncleans are tainting the waters. They are turning it into a swamp."

And with the word *swamp*, he growled and swung his outstretched arm across his windowsill, sending to the floor with a clatter his carved knickknacks and tchotchkes that he had whittled himself over the years.

Clawdy didn't know where to direct her attention. If she looked at the mess, it might anger him more. If she remained focused on his face, he might take that as aggressive. She let her gaze fall to her hands as she picked at a cuticle.

Her breath hitched in her throat when he covered the distance between them in three long but quick steps and grabbed her wrists. "I can turn a blind eye to your extracurricular boogying, but only because I know you have sworn your allegiance to Mother Dawn. We are a rare and dying breed, even among neuro-trancers."

Clawdy watched his face soften, which was his MO when he needed her on his side for anything. She never knew Cain to be scared, but something was tugging at his insides.

He still didn't seem to care that she had remained silent during his tirade because he finished with, "Praise Mother Dawn."

Clawdy bit the inside of her lip and contemplated not giving the appropriate response. Her stomach churned with the thought of her tongue forming words she no longer believed. But her fear of Cain's wrath overrode her own trepidation of creating a bigger issue between them.

"Mother Dawn be praised," she murmured as quietly as her stomach would allow her to but loud enough to not raise suspicion. "Are you gonna report losing a trancing today?"

"Don't be foolish. No one needs to know about that fool today."

"But if they find out, they'll excommunicate—"

Without warning—no part of his body language had indicated he would move—Cain slapped Clawdy across the face. A *thwomp* echoed in the room. "Get ready for bed. And never talk about today again. Or any future possible deserters either."

Clawdy rubbed her cheek where she had taken the brunt of the slap and felt heat radiating from her skin. She wiped a single tear from her eye—not from the pain but from the realization that the man she loved was no longer the same man. Cain had gone beyond the point of no return.

And she was scared to find out just how much more dangerous he could become.

10

Johnny Ray rubbed the stubble growing on his chin. A drone hovering outside the 10-19-94 subway entrance projected images onto the tele-skin in Mr. Broad's office. "I don't understand why the King of L.A. hasn't come out yet."

Mr. Broad punched his right fist into his left palm over and over. "Something has tripped him up."

Johnny Ray stepped toward the screen. "Impossible. He has a perfect track record. It's gotta be something else. Maybe he hasn't engaged yet. Biding his time."

Mr. Broad turned to glare at his assistant. "I think maybe your golden boy has finally become too old or too cocky for his own good."

"But they are teenagers!" Johnny Ray didn't mean for his voice to crack. "He's the king, for Mother Dawn's sake."

Mr. Broad turned fully to face Johnny Ray behind him. "Now I gotta send in someone else to do the king's original job and also maybe even save him."

Johnny Ray stepped backward. "Just … give him a little more time. You don't know what his plans are. Just because he didn't go down there and blow them all away doesn't mean he's not working his magic."

"Blowing them away was *exactly* what I wanted him to do," Mr. Broad growled. "So, either you didn't properly relay that information to him, or he's losing his touch."

Johnny Ray's gaze darted off Mr. Broad's face and onto the tele-skin behind his boss. He watched the stillness of the drone hovering high above platform 10-19-94. Something deep inside him felt wrong. Some itch in his brain was signaling that the King of L.A. had run into something unexpected.

"Lancelot," Mr. Broad called out into office.

"Yes, sir?"

"Are the Chameleon twins on the net?"

Silence filled the office while Lancelot searched to see if the two assassins had activated their availability status within the grid.

"Do you think that's wise," Johnny Ray asked, "after what happened last time we used them?"

"You don't think I have lost sleep over that night?" Mr. Broad answered in a whisper. "It haunts me every day, but they reconciled and cleared their credentials." Mr. Broad met Johnny Ray's gaze. "Everyone deserves a second chance, don't they? Or are you a hypocrite?"

Johnny Ray pursed his lips as memories of Mr. Broad giving him a second chance so many years ago ran through his head. Memories of when Cyber-Corp was still a start-up company and when Mr. Broad still went by his first name. A time before the megacorporations owned the government. Had Mr. Broad not given Johnny Ray that second chance, he probably would have visited a neuro-trancer years ago to send him trancing right the hell out of this dust bowl of a world.

Johnny Ray nodded in agreement, partly just so Mr. Broad would stop piercing holes in his face with his stare.

"Sir?" said the mechanicalized male voice through hidden speakers.

"Whatch'ya got, Lancelot?" Mr. Broad answered.

"The Chameleon twins are not on a mission, and both are on active status in the grid. Would you like me to summon them, sir?"

Mr. Broad paused and ripped a small piece of fingernail from his thumb with his teeth, his expression in deep and tortured thought. He glanced at Johnny Ray, maybe for one last piece of input from his associate.

Johnny Ray nodded once and answered for his boss, "Yes, Lancelot. Make the call."

"Very good, sirs."

*****

Johnny Ray pressed his forehead against the office window that overlooked the pathway below, waiting for the Chameleon twins to come into view from the Brundle Teleporter around the corner. At least he hoped Lancelot had reinstated their certificates to use Cyber-Corp's transports—after the investigation had cleared them from any wrongdoing in that fiasco last year that left so, so many factory workers dead and even more Synchestria Implants destroyed.

The sight of the two men, walking in perfect sync, around the corner and into view brought Johnny Ray from his memories. He watched the tops of their perfectly bald and shiny heads bounce with each step. Both clad in orange leather jackets, orange pants, orange cowboy boots. The twins alleged they were five feet tall, but Johnny Ray thought they were giving themselves half an inch on that claim.

As they disappeared below through the front doors, Johnny Ray's last thought concerning the twins was how they were the epitome of the adage *size doesn't matter*. If not for that factory mishap last year, Johnny Ray would go as far as to say the Chameleon twins might even rival the King of L.A. himself.

"Sir, the twins have arrived."

"Thank you, Lancelot. Unlock all the doors leading up here and instruct them to come up."

"Yes, sir."

Mr. Broad shot Johnny Ray a quick glance, then refocused on the tele-skin covering the far wall to watch for any movement exiting the targeted subway.

A few moments later, his office door opened, and the twins entered.

Johnny Ray stepped aside, to give himself more space from the assassins. They stood next to each other, shoulder to shoulder, not just twins genetically, but they mirrored each other in clothes, full orange beards, and baldness. Neither had a visible identifying birthmark or mole, so it was impossible to know which one to address with a name. Johnny Ray realized he didn't even *know* their names—first or last—nor if they even *had* names. They just were the Chameleon twins. Plain and simple.

"It's nice to see you again, Mr. Broad," the one on the left said, while the one on the right folded his arms.

"I wouldn't have called you if I didn't think it was dire."

"We appreciate you reinstating our creds at Cyber-Corp," the rightmost twin said. "The company exonerated our actions at the factory, but that doesn't mean you, yourself, have forgiven us."

"Do you need my forgiveness to accept a job?"

The one on the left smacked his lips. "We don't need anything except credits to accept a job. Yet what I think my brother is getting at is that it's against the assassin creed for us to work for someone who holds grudges against us."

Johnny Ray chortled from where he stood near the corner.

"Got something to say, Johnny Ray-gun?" asked the twin on the right.

"You guys and your creeds crack me up. The King of L.A. doesn't subscribe to a creed. Who even wrote this so-called creed?"

"Mother Dawn herself bestowed it upon all assassins centuries ago."

Johnny Ray shook his head and rubbed one of his eyes.

"And the self-appointed King of L.A. is a hack," one of the twins added.

Mr. Broad cleared his throat and shot Johnny Ray a warning to quit it. "I have forgiven you, both of you, for the factory incident. In fact, this main factory is the reason I called you. And, coincidentally, the King of L.A."

One of the twins snickered. "Told you. Hack."

Mr. Broad continued without acknowledging the comment. "The drone hasn't picked up any movement."

One of the twins squinted. "Is that the subway tunnels?"

Mr. Broad nodded and quickly checked his gold-chained pocket watch. "The last time we had cyberpunks squatting in the tunnels, they hit a factory shortly afterward." Mr. Broad pointed to a large structure farther down the screen. "We sent the King of L.A. to dispose of whomever is down there, but we think"—he eyed Johnny Ray—"something has happened to him."

"So, we're cleaning up his mess *and* completing his mission?" one of the twins asked.

"If that's what you need to tell yourself to get it done," Johnny Ray said from the corner.

"And what do you want us to do with the king?"

"He's not part of your mission. I guess, use discretion," Mr. Broad said and shrugged.

Johnny Ray didn't like the way both twins grinned when they turned to leave the office.

11

After Adam and Mony dragged the intruder into Adam's bedroom/office, they sat him against a wall, the thick wire pinning his arms behind him and binding his ankles together.

"I'll watch him," Mony said to Adam. "You should go out and check on the others,"

He nodded once and strode out the door and across the platform toward the sobbing coming from his friends. Venus's back was to him, her shirt stained a light crimson from Maggie's wounds. Adam stopped next to her and surveyed Maggie's body. Three clipper holes marked each place the rounds had gone through her.

Adam finally felt the adrenaline dump exit his veins, and he shook. He tried to stop his hands and legs from trembling, but it was futile. He dropped to a knee alongside Cherie and put a hand on Maggie's remaining cheek. He ground his teeth and forced his jaw to stop clenching, afraid he would break some of his teeth.

"I'm going to kill that junkie," he growled.

Venus laid a hand on his shoulder, and, when he looked up at her, she whispered, "We need to decide what to do with Maggie."

Adam sighed and fixed his gaze on Maggie's body again.

"Any ideas?" Jonesy asked the group.

"Where would Maggie want to be buried? If burials were still legal," Adam quipped.

"If someone catches us burying a body, that's five years minimum incarceration," Jonesy said.

"But we can't report it," Venus said. "That would out all of us."

"I don't plan to just leave her outside for them to find and to randomly dispose of her body," Adam said. "Plus it'll raise too many questions about where she came from, and we'll have to find a new hideout."

Adam caught Cherie glancing down the train tracks and into the void. "What are you thinking?" Adam asked her.

Cherie redirected her attention to Adam. "Maggie always loved the darkness of the tunnels. Plus it's quiet and peaceful there. She spent her life living in silence. I think she would want to stay that way."

Adam ran his tongue along the top row of teeth and sighed. "Thoughts? Anyone?"

He watched them shake their heads, and Venus said, "I think Maggie would approve." Then she flung a fist into her mouth to bite on her knuckles, stifling a growing sob that threatened to escape her throat.

"All right. Let's do this carefully." Adam tucked his hands underneath Maggie's ankles. "Jonesy, you got her shoulders?"

Jonesy nodded, and the two teens carried Maggie's body off platform 10-19-94 and onto the train tracks. They didn't stop walking or set Maggie down until the low lights from the platform were just a speck in the distance.

01100000111100011101 1100

Adam stalked into his office-turned-bedroom and snatched the thin, spinney trinket from his desk that he had found during their last raid. He held it now to keep his hands busy and preoccupied from strangling the intruder tied up on the floor.

The intruder slowly inclined his chin to focus on Adam—either because it was painful to move or because he wanted to intimidate the teen. Adam didn't know and didn't quite care.

Adam remained standing, staring at the man on the floor, while his fingers played with the object of the ancient ones. He needed to get control over his breathing—and emotions—before he questioned this man. Most likely a junkie, since the man wasn't fighting or trying to escape the wires. He just bore his stare from his one good eye into Adam's face.

Then he spoke. "I didn't expect them to find you living in the subway."

Adam tilted his head. "You don't get to freely talk. Do it again, and I'll kick in your jaw."

The intruder shifted his weight and eyed the object in Adam's hand but didn't obey the order. "Fidget spinner."

Adam ground his teeth and pulled his foot back to kick. "What'd you call me?"

The intruder chuckled, carefree and nonchalant. "What is in your hand. It's called a fidget spinner—a device to help people stay focused, during the Age of Destruction. I can tell you don't know what it is by how you're holding it."

Adam slowly lowered his foot and looked at Mony, who stood wide-eyed across the room. "You better start talking, or I'll kill you."

The intruder furrowed his brows. "I am a freedom fighter, like you kids." He scanned them with his one good eye. "But the rebellion needs money to survive. None of us have the Synchestria Implants—that would go against everything we're fighting against—but we also need to stay underground. Like you guys. So I hide in plain sight, by being available to the megacorporations as an assassin for hire. It takes more courage to infiltrate the system and to blow it up from the inside than to stand outside and throw rocks at its windows."

Unprompted, Mony kicked the intruder's knee as hard as she could. He flinched but did not have enough slack in the wire to reach for his knee. "Is that what you call what you did to Maggie? Courage? You slimy piece of—"

Adam raised a hand to interrupt Mony. "How did you know we were down here?"

Mony slapped her thighs in frustration. "C'mon, Adam. Seriously? This turd has probably been spying on us. He's probably been living in the darkness, watching and listening. Doesn't take a genius to figure that out."

Adam shook his head to clear his brain. Mony was right; Adam couldn't believe he hadn't originally assumed that this man had been spying on them. He had let the man derail him with such simple facts that anyone who had been watching would have known.

"How long have you been watching us?" Adam asked.

The intruder shook his head and snickered. "I found out that you kids were down here about an hour ago. When Cyber-Corp sent me down here to kill all of you."

"Prick," Mony said and stomped on the intruder's knee again.

The man grimaced this time and sucked in his lips. "But when I take a job that involves killing anyone who is also fighting for the rebellion, I recruit them and get them to safety, then report back to the hiring agency that I've killed them."

"How did they find us?"

"A drone," the man answered.

"We didn't see any drones down here. Why wouldn't it have stayed to confirm you actually killed us? Seems convenient that it's no longer here."

"They can't afford to be tied to the murdering of teens. No witnesses. No evidence. So, no cameras near the kill zone. They wait and hide far away to assess the aftermath."

Adam felt he finally had control over his emotions, as calmness engulfed him. He squatted onto his haunches and surveyed the man's features—the color of his hair, the wrinkles on his face, the long scar traveling down an eyelid that concealed an empty socket. "I have never seen anyone with white hair. From aging, at least."

"And I'm sure you've never seen anyone with different-colored eyes than orange," the man replied. "Yet here you are. The blue-eyed wonder. Makes both of us special."

When Venus entered, Adam looked toward the doorway.

Venus announced, "Jonesy and Cherie want to wait outside this office in case he somehow gets out of this room alive."

"What did you guys do with his clipper?"

"Jonesy has it," Venus said.

"Tell him that, if this man somehow gets out of this room, to shoot him with it."

Venus stuck her head outside the door, and Jonesy yelled, "Message received, loud and clear!"

Adam refocused on the man.

"C'mon, Adam. Let me shoot him!" Jonesy yelled from the platform.

"Hey, Adam?" Cherie yelled from near Jonesy. "Ask him if he was hiding out with any other friends."

Adam took his focus off the intruder and glanced at the doorway leading to the platform. "Why?"

"Because two men are walking down the stairs. Twins, I think. And they look angry."

12

Clawdy had forced herself to stay awake, staring ceilingward and replaying the moments of the day in her head. The room was dark and silent, Cain's breathing keeping time for her. When his breathing turned to snoring, she knew he was deep asleep, and she chanced slipping from the bed. Slowly she slithered her body in small inch-length movements to not wake him, until she planted her foot on the floor, and she let her torso clear the edge of the bed.

Clawdy stood and remained motionless for a minute to ensure she had not woken Cain. Satisfied he would not wake, she padded toward the door, held her breath when she turned the knob, and stealthily cracked it open just wide enough for her to blade through.

Once on the other side of the door and in the hallway, she secured it with as little noise as possible, then headed for Judas's room in the other barracks. She pushed through the front doors and traversed the hallway, until she reached Judas's door. She knocked quietly, so as not to alarm or to alert his neighbors on either side of him.

No answer.

She rapped a little harder.

From inside, she heard, "Hold on!"

The door swung open, revealing a disheveled and confused Judas. A laser-beam focus overcame his expression when he saw her reddened cheek. He grabbed Clawdy's wrist and pulled her inside his room.

He closed the door and faced her. "What on Mother Dawn's orange earth happened to you?"

Clawdy shook her head, afraid and unable to say it aloud. Unable to say his name right now.

"Did Cain do this to you?"

She nodded and put her face in her hands. Sobs racked her body as her shoulders curved inward.

Judas put an arm around her and led her to sit on the end of his bed.

She pulled her face from her hands and wiped her eyes with her sleeve. "He lost a trancing today."

Judas cocked his head in confusion. "He … didn't report losing one today."

When Clawdy started talking, she couldn't stop. All the day's events poured from her like a waterfall.

After she finished, Judas sat next to her on the bed. "He can be disbarred from trancing due to the failure to report. And he can be excommunicated for hitting you."

"I know." She sniffled.

"We have him on two egregious charges, both with separate punishments. And they could get you for being an accessory."

"I–I didn't do anything to help him lose the trancing!"

"No, but you knew about it, and you knew he never reported it. And it sounds like he has no plans to."

"But I'm telling *you*."

"And by doing so, you've put me in a precarious position because, if I don't report it, then I'm also an accessory." Judas grabbed her hands and offered her a warm smile. "I think you came to tell me because deep down you're wrestling with your own demons regarding Cain, and you want him gone."

Clawdy wanted to tell Judas that her demons didn't reside with Cain but with her wavering faith in Mother Dawn. But that would surely get her barred from trancing as well. So, until she was unequivocally sure in her heart of hearts that Mother Dawn was a farce, Clawdy would keep her doubts to herself.

"If I can talk him into reporting it tomorrow, do you think they will still give him the maximum sentence?"

Judas leaned back on his hands. "I'm sure there will be an investigation as to why it took him a day, when mandatory reporting is supposed to happen within the hour, but I could see them going easier on him."

Clawdy nodded. "Thank you. Please give me the opportunity to talk him into it before you say anything."

Judas took her hands in his. "I'm not here to see anyone get punished. However, we do have rules for a reason, and they exist for the betterment of the neuro-trancer sect. The community is more important than the individual person. Now, what shall we do about that nasty bruise that's forming on your cheek?"

Clawdy slid her hands from Judas's grasp and rubbed where it still stung. "That's between me and Cain. I know it's yet another rule he broke, but please respect me enough to handle this on my own."

Judas inclined his chin and took a short inhale through his nose. "Fair enough. Come on. I'll walk you back."

Standing from the bed, she said, "Oh, you don't have to do that."

"I insist. You owe me, if I'm gonna keep my mouth shut about this."

Relinquishing, she headed for the door, with Judas in tow. They made the short walk to her building, and he followed her down the hallway toward her door. Clawdy's heart jumped when she had an awful realization. What if

Judas had insisted to escort her back so he could confront Cain?

She spun to face him, and he almost walked right into her. "I'm just right there. This is fine. Thank you for listening."

Judas half closed one eye and scrutinized her. "I feel like you're trying to get rid of me."

She shook her head and shrugged. "Nope. Just don't want to inconvenience you any further."

He looked over her head at her closed door, then back at her. "Okay. Tomorrow though. Right? If he hasn't reported it by the end of the day, I will."

"Right." She nodded once.

He turned to leave but stopped and faced her again. "And you do know I'm not doing this because I dislike him. It's the right thing to do." He took her hands in his and softened his expression. "The rules are to keep us safe and to maximize the praise we give to Mother Dawn."

Clawdy heard her door open behind her, and it didn't even register that she was still holding Judas's hands when she watched Cain enter the hallway. Blood rushed to her ears as her heart exploded in fear, and the world became muffled.

The two men locked gazes, and only then did Judas release Clawdy's hands. She stepped backward instinctively, until the hallway wall pressed against her. She watched Cain ball his hands into fists and didn't even realize he had traveled the short length of the hallway, until he had Judas on the floor, pounding his face.

Clawdy screamed and lunged at her partner, colliding with him like a bull and sending them sprawling across the floor.

Judas took the opportunity to get to his knees and use the split second of confusion to get atop Cain and pin him down. "Don't struggle, and I won't hurt you," Judas growled.

Clawdy picked herself up from the floor and stood over the two men. The door next to them opened, and a fellow neuro-trancer poked out their head.

"Unless you want to be a part of this, get back in your room," Judas barked at the man.

The door slammed shut twice as fast as it had opened.

"Listen, Cain. I am going to let you up. And if you so much as flinch in my direction, I will lay you out and report you to the elders in the morning. Do you understand?"

Cain turned his head and spat blood onto the hallway floor. "Praise Mother Dawn."

Judas slowly swung a leg off the neuro-trancer's body and rose to his feet. He stepped backward to give Cain space to get his footing. "Mother Dawn be praised," Judas replied, then regarded a trembling Clawdy. "You okay?"

She nodded and pressed her palm to her chest to will her heart to slow to a normal pace.

"I know what it looked like when you opened the door, but it's not what you're thinking," Judas said. "Clawdy just came to me for some advice."

"Is that so?" Cain said in a growl and shot eye daggers at her. "What kind of advice would she be looking for?"

Clawdy's gaze darted to Judas, hoping the man wouldn't reveal their conversation. She wanted to deal with her partner on her own terms and timeline.

Judas took an aggressive step forward. "What she should do when she knows a neuro-trancer has lost a trancing. And didn't report it to the elders."

Cain lowered his chin and glared at her from underneath his eyebrows.

Clawdy's vision blurred with terror and more adrenaline, and she couldn't help but think Judas was doing this on purpose—putting her in unnecessary danger—but for what reason?

"We will speak about this in private," Cain finally said to her and grabbed one of her wrists.

Clawdy was too stunned to react, which was good. She didn't know what reaction other than submission wouldn't make him angrier. She didn't even look back to see what Judas was doing while her partner dragged her down the hallway and into their room.

Cain slammed the door, trapping the two of them inside. And she knew she was now completely at Cain's mercy.

0110000111110001110111 00

"Praise Mother Dawn," Cain said, more as a growl, glaring at his companion.

Clawdy focused on the floor and found herself taking a step backward.

"I said … *praise Mother Dawn*. Don't anger her by not responding correctly."

Clawdy raised her gaze and met his eyes. Her teeth ground, and her lips pulled taut with anger and fear. "I can't stomach the thought of saying those words to you ever again."

Cain tilted his head and squinted at her. "Are you denouncing her?"

Clawdy glanced out the single window at the darkness outside and realized she was on the precipice of either making a life-changing decision or submitting to him and letting everything return to chaotic normalcy.

She stormed forward and tried to pass him for the door, but he snatched her wrist and spun her toward him. Their faces were so close that she could feel the exhales from his nose on her cheek. Her body trembled, but she kept eye contact, hoping to show some aggression.

"Where do you think you're going?"

"Away from you, from this place, and Mother Dawn's unhealthy hold on your common sense."

"She has promised me a special place in Shangri-la. She approves of my work here."

Clawdy snatched her wrist free from his grip. "You are so delusional." She stepped toward the door. "How did you understand her, when you said she spoke in tones?"

Clawdy wanted to keep him answering questions while she inched toward freedom. If she could distract him long enough and get close enough to the exit, she could turn and run the rest of the way, hopefully closing the door on him in time to buy her some distance. She was sure that, in an all-out sprint, she could outrun him on even her worst day.

"How did the ancients understand their form of communication that they called Morse Code, *huh*? Wasn't that all just tones?"

Shuffle, shuffle.

"Because they created what the tones signified themselves. You're talking about a foreign language, with no legend to use to transcribe what the tone represents."

A bit closer. Shuffle, shuffle.

"When the layers of tones congregated into that single tone and that *bing, bing, bing* noise, all her meanings opened up to me."

Clawdy chanced a peek at the door just to size up the distance she had to cover. She thought if she threw one more question at him, she would count to one so he would be in the most-distracted state of thinking of an answer, then she would bolt.

"Why do you think she hasn't spoken to you since? Or has she?"

Question out. *One* … Run!

Clawdy grabbed the knob and pulled, all in one swift motion, went through the door and felt it bounce off his outstretched palms. But that was okay. She was in the hallway, and her shoes gained purchase on the floor. She felt herself pulling away from him. Could see him getting farther behind in her mind's eye. He was slow and lethargic; she was quick and coordinated.

Clawdy exploded through the front doors into the open fields and knew positively that Cain could never catch up to her now. She veered away from Judas's barracks, not wanting to run into that little prick again. She shook her head as she ran and almost chuckled at the thought that she had trusted her safety with him. Deity junkies were all they were. So consumed by *needing* a higher power to exist that they didn't care who they trampled on, as long as they could justify that they did it in *her* name.

Clawdy's legs felt good, strong. She enjoyed the adrenaline coursing through her veins as she sprinted across the field toward … toward where? What would she do now? She couldn't stay in the commune. She would have to make it on the outside herself—somewhere Cain could never find her.

Not that he would leave the commune to search for her. She knew that. He didn't love her; he just liked controlling her. She was certain another weak-minded drifter would stumble across the commune soon, be subjected to neuro-trancer brainwashing, then sent out to provide trancing to anyone who happened to have enough credits to pay for the process—to escape this dustbowl of a world prematurely to reach Shangri-la in the only way Mother Dawn approved.

The recordkeepers swore that what the ancients had called a *suicide* hadn't occurred in hundreds of years. Not since they had discovered trancing and had birthed the sect of people who devoted their lives to administering the process, devoted their lives to help those who were suffering. At least, that was what Clawdy thought neuro-trancers were supposed to do and was why Mother Dawn had created neuro-trancers—to give those in anguish the only approved way out.

She realized her legs were bringing her to the trancing complex. She saw it in the distance, growing larger with each stride. As the building came closer into view, her thoughts spiraled further into forbidden territories for a neuro-trancer. If Mother Dawn approved trancing, gave the process her blessing—heck, it was said that many, many people all over the world had discovered trancing after hearing Mother Dawn's instructions on how to create the serum—then why did it cost so much? Why did power and money dictate who could utilize Mother Dawn's gift to the human race?

The large structure loomed in front of Clawdy now. She had always heard about all those people so long ago who all simultaneously heard Mother Dawn's voice, calling for them to create the serum, but Clawdy didn't know *how* they had heard Mother Dawn. Clawdy tucked that thought into her back pocket and told herself to remember to one day ask about that—if she got out of this situation alive.

What she needed to do next played out in front of her as clear as day. The plan was almost palpable. Almost as if Mother Dawn herself was formulating her thoughts.

Clawdy closed her eyes, made a fist, turned her head away, and smashed one of the windows to the trancing complex.

13

"You might want to untie me and give me my clipper back, if you don't want to die right now," the intruder said with zero inflection in his tone.

Adam shivered at the man's calmness, which made it feel even more diabolical. But he laughed instead of submitting to the fear. "Why on Mother Dawn's orange earth would we *ever*—"

Clipper bolts shattered all the windows in the office as Cherie and Jonesy ducked and ran into the room and closed the door behind them.

"You literally have ten seconds before all of you are dead," the murderous intruder said.

Adam glared at Venus for any sign of what she might be thinking.

She shook her head. "I still think they are with him."

The five cyberpunks had their backs against the wall below the windows for cover, with their bound intruder across the room, against the far wall.

"I would say you are down to eight seconds," the man said.

Jonesy turned to face the wall and slowly raised himself until his eyes crested the windowsill to look onto the platform. "They are just standing there," he whispered and set the man's clipper on the sill to take aim.

"You have bought yourself some more seconds there, kiddo, but trying to get a shot off on them would spell certain death before you could even scream."

Adam sighed heavily as he surveyed the tied man on the floor. "Who are they?" he mouthed more than spoke.

"Assassins. Sent to wipe out you guys. Wipe out all cyberpunks."

Adam leaned forward and took the clipper from Jonesy's hands. "Isn't that what you are?"

The intruder nodded. "According to the megacorporations, yes. However, if you had trusted me a few minutes ago about being with you guys and not against you, we would have been long gone before the twins got here. But now they're between us and getting out." He tilted his head toward the closed door. "So, either untie me and let me handle them or die."

Venus spun her head toward him. "Untie you so then *you* can finish the job before they can? I'm sure the first one to kill us gets the prize. Do we look stupid?"

The intruder grinned, and it sent an even worse chill down Adam's spine than his stoic speaking tone. "The difference is, the twins won't care about finding Adam. I do. After I shot your friend—which I am wholeheartedly sorry about, but you know danger comes with our uprising—do you really think I allowed you bunch of *kids* to overpower me enough to incapacitate me? I knew it was the only way you guys would pause long enough so I could talk to you, if you felt safe in the room with me. This"— he lowered his gaze to his bound wrists—"was my backup plan."

Jonesy lowered his body to the floor and whispered, "They started coming this way again."

"You're back to the clock reading only seconds," the intruder said.

Adam faced Venus, needing to see something in her expression to help him decide what to do. But *he* didn't need to see anything in *her* eyes.

She saw something in *his* eyes and crawled like she was on fire toward the intruder, pulled her retractable knife from her pocket, and, to everyone's astonishment, cut the wire around the intruder's arms.

"Give him the clipper," she whispered as she moved to snip the wire binding his ankles.

Adam snapped from his shock of seeing her free the man who had just killed Maggie and slid the clipper across the floor, where it landed against the man's thigh. The intruder, now completely freed, snatched the weapon from the floor and scooted toward the closed door.

"Stay against that wall," the man ordered them. He put his own back against the entrance to the office. He clasped the clipper, only half activated and charged, and pointed at the shot-out windows above where the teens sat.

Adam scanned his friends' expressions, all marred with a mixture of fear and a little bit of curiosity.

"If I can't see you," spoke one of the twins from the other side of the closed door, "then you can't see me. Your ways of the old arts have failed you finally, haven't they, Peasant of L.A.? Now we'll issue in a new breed."

Adam watched the intruder smirk and thought he chortled under his breath.

"You're just a watered-down version of us old-guard warriors."

"*Ahh*, so the Peasant of L.A. does live and breathe. Thought maybe these twerps had bested you," the man replied. "And, if memory serves me correctly, you're the last of the dinosaurs. Once we dispatch you, your kind will be extinct."

The intruder made eye contact with Adam to ensure the teen was focusing on him, then pointed to the desk in the room, signaling for all of them to get behind it for cover.

The cyberpunks crawled in a single file from the windows and got behind the desk. Adam was thankful for a little more concealment but didn't like not seeing what the intruder was doing.

And then the unmistakable sounds of clipper rounds filled the office.

0110000111110001110111100

One of the twin's silhouettes graced the side of the open window, and the King of L.A. raised the clipper and steadied his breath. Even if he could only retire one twin by surprise, he was confident he could take out the other twin in a good old-fashion firefight. These twins were the hacks—all talk and no talent.

The short man didn't advance any farther into the open window space. Probably didn't want to get caught in the fatal funnel, the King of L.A. assumed. They might be hacks, but they weren't stupid.

Then the twin showed just enough of his bald head where the King of L.A. thought he could take a kill shot. He squeezed the trigger and watched the man's head jerk sideways, out of sight, and a barrage of clipper rounds filled the room from the other side of the shot-out window. The King of L.A. had no way of knowing just yet if he had killed the twin or had just scratched the man. Did those rounds come from his brother or the first twin?

He rolled across the floor and landed directly under the open windows, where the teens had been sitting just a few moments ago.

"You shot off my blasted ear!"

That gave the King of L.A. his answer as to whether he had killed one of the assassins.

His gaze shot to the closed door. One could come from above him through the window and the other through the door, and while he was still confident in his skillset, he doubted whether his old bones and battle-worn muscles could move fast and limber enough to take out both twins if they entered simultaneously.

He decided to buy some time to formulate a plan by trash talking. "Not fast enough for this old geezer, I see."

The King of L.A. waited and listened to the wounded man's groans while he was probably tending to his injured ear. If an ear was still there at all.

"I guess you newbies are too concerned with how you look when on the job than actually getting the job done, huh?" he taunted. "The new breed is all soft."

The silence from outside the office made him uneasy. He couldn't hear the wounded assassin moaning anymore, and the sound of footfalls were nonexistent. Were they hiding? Or plotting? Or had they retreated to regroup? That would give him and the cyberpunks enough time to clear the subway and to get somewhere safe before the twins returned.

But no. Retreating was not in their MO. Not in *any* assassin's MO. This smelled like a trap.

The King of L.A. checked the bottom of the clipper for the orange LED readout—ninety rounds left before he would need to recharge the weapon. If he couldn't retire these two twerps within ninety rounds, he would hang up his hat as an assassin. That would just be pathetic. He had a good notion to use the remaining rounds on Mr. Broad, after setting him up like this.

The Chameleon twins. What an insult. The good ole days were really dead.

Then he heard boots shuffling on the platform. They were trying to be stealthy. *Trying*. What a joke. Laughable, really. He was just thankful the teens had obeyed and went behind the desk. He cared what could happen to the teens, but he also accepted that they might lose some more of the group before this was over—that was the risk they all knew before any of them became freedom fighters—save for the blue-eyed kid. He was the prize. He was to be guarded and protected at all costs.

A crunch of broken glass under a boot sounded right outside the open window. The King of L.A. now knew the twins had been creeping back to the office. And he was certain one would take the door, while the other took the window. He glanced at the desk and thought, *But the kid will be exposed*. He played the scene in his head to ensure he wasn't missing anything—any movement that would be fatal if missed. If the kid doesn't get hit in the crossfire, then it's a win.

The King of L.A. lunged across the room, revealing his tactical position, and dropped behind the desk with the teens. He hunched over and slid the desk with all his strength across the office and against the door to cut off that entryway. He then frantically pointed at the desk to signal for them to get behind it again.

The sound of a body slamming against the door happened simultaneously as clipper rounds came through the open window, just as the King of L.A. had expected. Maybe he wasn't getting rusty just yet.

He calculated that he might be able to jump through the window space, take out whichever twin was there, then cut the corner while still firing, hopefully retiring the second twin before he could turn to face the King of L.A.

He glanced at the prize, and the blue-eyed boy's face looked almost expressionless. Almost. A touch of fear resided in his eyes. And the King of L.A. needed that fear to remain. That fear would keep the unrealized hero alive until he could get the boy topside.

The King of L.A. nodded once at the boy to let him know he would protect him—that the boy could trust him. He waited for the prize to nod in return. Then the King of L.A. spun, placed a hand on the windowsill, and jettisoned himself out the window, firing clipper rounds as fast as his finger could pull. At nothing.

The rounds hit the wall across the platform, across the train tracks, in the distance, exploding in orange flashes where they struck.

He quickly darted around the corner, firing another series of rounds, maybe getting both twins. He watched those rounds strike the wall just above where Jonesy had cooked stew a few hours earlier.

He pressed his backside against the office door, scanning the platform for movement. For signs of the twins. Half an ear and the puddle of blood on the ground from the injured twin caught his one good eye. He trailed the blood with his gaze, away from the office, and toward the steps.

They had retreated. And very anticlimactically too. The King of L.A. wouldn't be lying if he said he was somewhat disappointed.

Or the uninjured twin could still be down here, hiding and stalking its prey. The King of L.A. had to decide whether it was safe enough to move the cyberpunks from the subway or to bide his time to ensure they were alone. He also realized that Mr. Broad had probably disabled the King of L.A.'s Brundle Teleporter access, so they would be huffing it on foot from here on out.

A blinding pain seared through his left hand as a flash of orange exploded from the train tracks. Sneaky bastard was hiding behind the rails. The King of L.A. spun off the wall and fired a handful of rounds toward where the blast had come from. He ducked while he ran, following the bloody trail of the earless twin, and stopped behind a large pillar on the platform. He tracked the blood droplets with his gaze and saw they had gone up the stairs to the world above. Coward.

He inched toward the edge of the pillar so he could see the spot on the tracks where the flash had originated. He squinted in the darkness but couldn't decipher a person there. He would have seen them if they had popped up and relocated. Unless they were crawling along the tracks, then he wouldn't see them until they fired again. At least he could see them if they tried to breach the office again. So at least the boy was safe. For now.

The King of L.A. shook his left hand to ward off the pain. At least all his fingers were still intact, but blood soaked every inch of his hand. This cat-and-mouse game had to end. He had to draw out the remaining twin onto the tracks. Knowing he didn't have to worry about two targets anymore, he spun off the pillar and ran, slaloming toward the office, scanning the tracks with the muzzle of his clipper.

Orange blasts exploded from farther down the tracks, and the King of L.A. dropped to the ground as rounds went over his head—rounds that would have found their mark. He rolled and hunched as he ran and fired in the vicinity of where the prone twin was. The King of L.A. knew he had to keep track of how many rounds he used. Ninety seemed overkill a few moments ago. Not so much now.

He reached the shot-out window of the office and placed his back against the wall, then spoke through the empty window. "We're gonna make a break for it. One of them already took off. The other is lying on the train tracks."

Venus stuck out her head from behind the desk. "That doesn't seem like the best idea."

"Fine. That assassin out there is after you guys. Not me. I'm just collateral damage or something in their way. If I leave, he won't follow me. He'll come straight in here and just open fire, left to right, until you're all dead. I'm risking my hide right now to get you out of here. Do you, missy, have a better plan?"

Adam stood. "No. We'll go with you. But I will have a lot of questions once we're out of this."

"I'm sure you will. We're covered here against this wall. Climb through and line up behind me."

He watched the cyberpunks cross the office space and helped them, one by one, roll through the shot-out window. When all five of them were lined up behind him, he said, "That first pillar on the platform is wide enough for us to get behind. I'll go first and light up the tracks with the clipper. You run behind me and stop behind that pillar."

"Why not just keep running up the stairs?" Mony asked.

He looked at her and pointed into the depths of the darkness of the tunnel beyond. "Because I don't know if he's relocated to a spot where he has a better shot if we kept going. He will fire when we start running. I want to reevaluate based on his position. But I promise you that it will be quick when we move again. When I point to the stairs, we run. Got it?"

The teens nodded.

"Okay. And Blue Eyes?"

"Adam."

"Okay. Adam? I want you to stay as close to my back as possible."

"Why him specifically?" Cherie asked.

The King of L.A. didn't answer.

14

Mr. Broad sighed, then dropped into his orange leather couch in his office. "What is going on down there?"

Johnny Ray knew it was rhetorical but felt the need to answer anyway. "Looks like a standoff."

Mr. Broad rubbed his face with his palm and groaned. "No way that the King of L.A. can outwit the Chameleon twins, right? He is aging. And slow. And there's *two* of them."

Johnny Ray poured himself half a glass of orange liquor, brought the cup to his lips, and took a sip. "None of this will matter when we finish the Synchestria mining."

Mr. Broad picked a piece of orange lint off his dress pants and let it fall to the carpet. "The slavebots need more testing. I can't afford one of them accidentally killing someone."

Johnny Ray turned on the couch to face his boss. "We have been developing these bots for almost a decade, as our own police force, for the purpose of never, ever having to hire people like the King of L.A. or the Chameleon twins again. If you don't think that *now* is the best time to activate them, just look at that tele-skin!" He pointed to the screen on the wall, showing what the drone's camera saw—a vacant subway entrance where something obviously had gone afoul. "We have been extracting the information from the Synchestria Implants for years. Years! And mapped all that data to build a police force that will never make a mistake."

Mr. Broad leaned over to the side table and poured himself a drink. "We're not the government. We're still a corporation. We must be careful in the public eye."

"We're more powerful than the government! We control what people see, hear, taste … think. We have given everyone a better life through making sure they only experience what they want to experience, using the Synchestria Implants. Could you imagine still living in an age where we had to decide what we liked? And now the slavebots will police exactly how the people want to be policed."

Mr. Broad took a long gulp of alcohol and set the glass on the table in front of him. He ran his fingers along his lips, deep in thought. "I want a demonstration."

Johnny Ray cocked his head. "I don't follow. A demonstration of what?"

Mr. Broad scooted closer to the edge of the couch and crossed his legs. "I want a controlled demonstration of the slavebots in a live scenario. They must be perfect in every way, or I will continue using human assassins. When we are ready to deploy the bots into the province, we must ensure there isn't panic. We need to document, with real-life examples, how safe they are and get that information to the public. It's a delicate dance to get the populace to except waking up one morning with never having a police force, to having dozens of ten-foot-tall bots patrolling every street in the provinces. It could either tip the scales in our favor and finally eradicate all government, giving us sole power of the country, or it could create outrage and pushback, which could be the spark the people need to desire governing bodies again."

Johnny Ray teepeed his hands in thought. "The introduction of the bots into society is the final stage in our takeover. We've gotten the people submissive and trusting enough, showing them how the Synchestria Implants can enhance their lives, that I think they will have more faith in us than you think."

"Don't underestimate the power of people when they feel they've been duped one too many times. The ancients had multitudes of real-life stories of their oppressed rising up to overtake an entity controlling them."

"But we're not controlling them, sir. We are giving them what they want, based on the data pooled from their Synchestria Implants. If I had an implant and my favorite ice cream was, I dunno, mint chocolate chip, wouldn't I want to know that mint chocolate chip ice cream was on sale at the market? Without the implants, they wouldn't know this. And hence they would miss out on things they love. The slavebots will do the same thing. They will give the people the policing they actually want, based on their data from their implants."

"But mint chocolate chip ice cream can't turn on you and accidentally kill you. It'll only take one misstep, and we will lose the trust of the people. And megacorporations will lose integrity—the same downfall that allowed us to supersede the government."

Johnny Ray sighed and checked his watch. "All right. I'll set up a practical exam, if you will, for the bots." A beat of silence passed before he added, "Or we could just deploy them now, programmed only to take down cyberpunk cells." He slowly turned his head to catch what expression his boss might have in response to that suggestion. "That could be our controlled experiment. See how they do with protection of the company's assets."

Mr. Broad snickered and raised his glass so Johnny Ray could clink his own in a cheers. "Whenever I wonder why I confide in you, you always reaffirm my confidence in you."

"Thank ya, sir."

"Lancelot?"

"Yes, sir?"

"Transmit a message to the Chameleon twins to disengage from their mission. We need these cyberpunks alive for our testing."

"Right away, sir."

Mr. Broad took a long swallow on his glass and smacked his lips. "Okay, let's stop fooling around with this soup-sandwich that's happening down there. Deploy a platoon of slavebots to wipe out all the cyberpunk cells. I think we can win the public's trust if they see the bots doing good first. The people will be less likely to panic when the bots arrive in droves in the communities."

"Heck, sir, they may even welcome them with open arms."

Mr. Broad pointed at his assistant, just as the early morning sun crested the horizon in the windows behind them. "That's the dream right there."

15

Clawdy snatched back her hand as fast as she could after punching out the window to the trancing complex, hoping she wouldn't get cut. She paused to listen for any alarms or sirens. She realized she had no idea if the building was armed with detection of break-ins. Maybe silent alarms were going off right now in the elders' quarters. She had no idea. So, she needed to move. Fast.

Clawdy climbed through the window and landed inside, her feet planted squarely. She was thankful that she didn't need the lights to navigate through the hallways and rooms; she knew the interior like the back of her hand.

Using the outlines and shadows of the corners and doorways, she maneuvered to her room. She took a breath and paused outside the door. She knew this would be the last time she would be inside her trancing station. A room that had been her sanctuary for so many years now. A room that had been a haven after a childhood of abuse and neglect. A room inside a commune that had accepted her like family from day one. A commune that had never judged, had trained her, and had given her the skillset and the know-how to become a neuro-trancer—the most elite being on the planet in Mother Dawn's eyes. And here she was, two steps from giving it all the middle finger and going rogue.

Had a neuro-trancer ever deserted before? She couldn't remember hearing stories of one. And what would the punishment be if she were caught? Would the elders handle it here on this plain, or would Mother Dawn handle it in Shangri-la?

Clawdy shook her head to clear her thoughts. That was a slippery slope if she stayed on that pathway of wondering. She bolted through the door and stormed to the cupboard. She rummaged around the bottom shelf for the orange duffel bag, then took as much trancing serum and syringes that she could and tossed them into the bag. When she had filled the bag—almost to the point of not being zipped— she flung it over her shoulder and exited her trancing station for the last time.

She did not want to go the way she had entered, in case a silent alarm had alerted someone who may be approaching from that side of the building, so she fled through the back hallways and out the rear door.

With no plan and no friends and no family but with a bag full of neuro-trancer tools, she headed toward life outside the commune, wondering how many credits she could make trancing on the streets. When she had been in high school, they had learned about something the ancients did called *prostitution*. She wondered if what she was about to do would be considered the same thing—except, instead of offering sex for money, she was offering an eternal trip to paradise. And wasn't that better?

While distracted with thoughts of the ancients, her strong legs had carried her past the borderline of the commune before she even knew it. And for the first time since she had been a teenager, Clawdy surveyed the landscape before her. Freedom in the form of a populated city, with an immeasurable number of potential patients and so, so many places to hide from the elders of the neuro-trancers.

16

The King of L.A. pointed to his good eye, then at the pillar, and gave the *go* sign. The assassin and the five cyberpunks scampered across the platform for the pillar, and orange LED-colored bolts fired from the darkness in the tunnel farthest from the stairs.

The King of L.A. turned and released a barrage of clipper rounds into the tunnel, the display on the weapon showing he was down to only twenty remaining rounds.

"Forget the pillar," he yelled as they ran. "Get up the stairs!" He ran forward but twisted his body backward to send a few rounds into the darkness.

The teens jumped the turnstiles and raced up the stairs, three steps at a time.

The King of L.A. slowed his pace so he was in the rear of the pack, where he could return fire if the Chameleon twin left his hiding spot and followed them to continue the assault. But nothing happened.

They reached the top of the stairs at street level, and Venus asked, "Why did he stop firing? And why isn't he following us?"

The King of L.A. searched the ground for the blood trail of the injured twin and saw it went down the pathway. "I don't know. Something doesn't feel right. I don't like any of this."

"We need to keep moving," Adam said.

The King of L.A. nodded in agreement as he turned to lead them farther into the city.

"Where are we going?" Cherie asked.

"We can't use any of the teleporters. I'm sure I have now been blacklisted from using them. Also Cyber-Corp would know you were in them with me. And you are their main target. We're gonna go to the Peppermint Lounge. A secret hideout is in the backroom that none of the megas knows about."

"We're gonna hide in the back of a pub?" Jonesy said more as a statement than a question.

The King of L.A. turned and walked backward to face the group. "It's not what you're thinking. It's its own ecosystem back there." He made eye contact with the prize. "You'll be safe there because we protect our own, like I tried to tell you from the beginning."

"And what about that drone you said would definitely be watching the aftermath? Your words not mine," Venus said.

"You guys keep your heads down so they can't get facial recognition on you and let me worry about what's in the sky."

01100001111000111011100

The twin's transmitter beeped twice. Lancelot was sending a message. Didn't Mr. Broad know the twin was hiding in the darkness, seconds from completing the mission once the group of cyberpunks headed for the exit? Seconds from taking them all down—and the washed-up old man too. He almost didn't check the message. Wanted to complete the mission first, then he would see what was so important. But this was a message from his employer. And, if he wanted to get paid, he needed to ensure there were no changes in the plan—especially since his brother was now somewhere dealing with possibly not having two ears anymore.

Abort.

That was all it said. Abort. That meant don't engage. Don't follow. Don't do anything, even after almost getting killed himself and his brother losing an appendage. Just … abort.

But a job was a job. And the assassin's creed dictated that the employer was the highest-ranking official of any mission. So, abort he must.

He replied to the message with, *Terrible timing. The brats and the idiot are going topside right now.*

He holstered his clipper and watched the teens and the old man run up the stairs. He hoped there was a good reason to abort and that the reason would include him somehow.

He didn't want to take the law into his own hands. Again.

0110000111111000111011100

The King of L.A. wasn't used to running along the pathways that once had been called *streets* during the Age of Destruction, his head on a swivel for incoming attacks, like he was some kind of criminal. He was used to being the hunter, not the hunted.

The cyberpunks followed him, block by block, like good ducklings. His aging legs and feet begged for a Brundle Teleporter, but he knew those days were over. Especially after tonight.

The King of L.A. kept scanning the skies for any sign of a Cyber-Corp drone. He knew their tactics so well that they had become predictable. He was sure Mr. Broad was watching them from above somehow, but, if they moved quickly and the kids kept their heads down, as he had instructed, he felt they had somewhat of a chance to reach their destination without it spotting them, especially with the lounge so close now.

The hole in his left hand had clotted, and the blood on his fingers had dried. He still needed to tend to his wound so it wouldn't get infected, but at least he wasn't losing blood anymore.

Without too much complaint from the teens behind him, they turned a corner and saw the Peppermint Lounge sign ahead. "Act calm, and no one say anything when we enter," he told the group. "They will not trust you until I vouch for you."

The King of L.A. watched the blue-eyed boy turn and give his lady friend a look. Obviously, they seemed to be in love. Just another thing for the King of L.A. to worry about. And he seriously wondered why he had volunteered for this job.

The King of L.A. pushed through the double orange doors into the Peppermint Lounge, his ducklings following, and strode to the bar counter as if he owned the joint. He went past the bar and reached for the orange curtain that separated the behind-the-bar area from the hidden rooms beyond, However, the barkeep stopped the King of L.A. in his tracks, wiping his hands across the orange dish towel flung across his shoulder, and surveyed the group of kids inside his pub.

"I know the rules," the King of L.A. said to intercept any comments from the barkeep. "But this is dire, and I'm calling *manifesto*."

The barkeep's face twitched when he heard the code word used in the underground to get everyone to the shelter in the wastelands. He hurried to the front double doors and locked them.

One asleep drunkard in the corner awoke from the noise and raised a hand to protest.

"We've called a manifesto!" the barkeep yelled at him.

Adam turned to face the drunk, feeling a bit of pity and wondering if the man had a Synchestria Implant—maybe that was how he had enough money to feed his addiction. The man nodded, and his gaze landed on Adam's eyes. The man stiffened, appearing cold-stone sober now, and a chill ran down Adam's spine at the way the patron regarded him.

Adam refocused on the King of L.A. when he spoke again; he seemed to somewhat revel in watching the barkeep try to comprehend why a bunch of cyberpunks were in his pub, escorted by an assassin.

"Before we say anything further," the barkeep said, eyeing the line of teens against the bar, "are all of you clean?"

"You can check our necks if you want to, but we're cyberpunks. No way we let them put those implants in us," Cherie answered.

The barkeep faced the King of L.A. "You're confident they're clean?"

The assassin rubbed his hands together and scanned his band of misfits. Then he nodded. "They're clean."

"All right. Let's go in the back and discuss why you shut down my pub tonight," the barkeep countered. He led the way behind the counter, the group following, through the orange curtains, which revealed a warehouse-size area, full of beds, food, water, and unfamiliar surgical machines. Small clusters of people milled about. "In the far back room. More privacy."

They entered a round office-like room, where the barkeep sat on a couch. He gestured for them to find seats among the many recliners and chairs. The King of L.A. closed the office door, and the barkeep's demeanor changed from one of someone who serves drinks to alcoholics to one who may have had some military training.

"If this is another false alarm, so help me Mother Dawn, I will rip your tongue out your mouth and hang you with it."

The teens remained silent and watched the assassin to see how he would respond.

The King of L.A. put his elbows on his knees and leaned forward. "First, I need to take care of this." He raised his left hand and showed the barkeep the clipper wound.

"We will, but you've survived this long without treatment, so you can go a bit longer, after you've explained why you triggered a manifesto." The man glared at the row of silent teens. "And brought *them* in here."

"Mr. Broad hired me to kill them. Of course I was going in to collect them for the cause." The King of L.A. darted the gaze from his one good eye at Adam to see if the boy had any reaction. He didn't. That was good. Maybe everything that had happened tonight had hardened the boy. He would need it to deal with what was to come. "But when I found them, I …"

The barkeep leaned forward. "You what?"

The King of L.A. now made eye contact with the prize's girlfriend. He knew once he said this next part, the teens might get heated again. He needed to play this safe.

"He means, he killed our deaf friend Maggie," Cherie finished.

The King of L.A. rested his knuckles against his closed lips, contemplating how to reveal the next part of what had happened. "The boy reacted as anyone would. He tried to neutralize the threat. And he did. Successfully."

The barkeep scooted closer to the edge of the couch and rested his chin on his two outstretched thumbs. "And how, pray tell, did this teen neutralize the most-experienced freedom fighter of our era?"

The King of L.A. looked at Adam but directed his statement to the barkeep. "You tell me."

The barkeep squinted and slid forward, almost to the point of falling off the couch, until his eyes widened. "Praise Mother Dawn."

"Mother Dawn be praised," the assassin mumbled.

The barkeep rose and approached the teen, never taking his gaze off the boy's ice-blue eyes. "*Manifesto* is right."

Venus grabbed Adam's hand for security when the barkeep crouched to meet the boy eye to eye.

The one-eyed assassin continued. "Cyber-Corp sent the Chameleon twins to finish the job and to probably knock me off too. At least that's what I assume Mr. Broad did after he realized I hadn't killed them all in the first thirty seconds of breaching their hiding place."

The barkeep spun to face the assassin. "And where are the twins now?"

"I got a good shot off one of them. He fled. The other just stopped shooting."

"Does Mr. Broad know we are dealing with"—he placed a hand on the side of Adam's face—"such delicate cargo?"

"I don't think so. Or he wouldn't have sent in the twins to finish the job."

"That works in our favor."

"Right. But I still don't know why the twin in the subway just gave up on us. He was obviously called off. But for what?"

"You are all safe here," the barkeep said. "Take any bed you like. Eat and drink as much as you like. Nobody is allowed back here who has an implant. That prevents them from tracking us."

"Sun is rising," the King of L.A. said. "Sounds counterintuitive, but we need a windowless area. So, *lights out* means *darkness*. Simulating nighttime. We all need some rest." The barkeep pointed to the next room. "Windowless."

The King of L.A. nodded. "Let's get some shuteye. We'll figure out what's going on tonight when we wake up."

He watched Venus lean into Adam's ear and say something.

"It's safe here, if that's what you're wondering. You're alive right now because this is a haven. You became cyberpunks to be part of an underground movement, right? You had no idea until right now how deep that movement goes. You were swimming in the kiddie pool, until tonight. Welcome to the deep end. And it's time you hung up your minnow hats and joined us sharks."

17

Johnny Ray got to his office, sat in his office chair, and activated his tele-skin, which, unlike his boss's, covered all four walls— a full 360 degrees of monitors. He had contemplated adding a screen to the ceiling for full immersion. Maybe when he got his bonus after the slavebots proved their usefulness.

The four walls now represented a map of the country, broken down into the four provinces—each province filling a screen. Dots littered the tele-skins, representing every human in the country who sported a Synchestria Implant— all ten million of those who had taken the huge payout that Cyber-Corp had offered to install a Synchestria Implant into their brains. Technically, the procedure injected the implant into the customer's neck, but the diodes found the electrical current inside the brain to reach the person's mind.

The Midwest Province was practically vacant, leaving thousands of miles of the country sparse and desolate. Most people had migrated to the two coasts decades ago. He thought it would benefit the country if the president just split up the Midwest Province and combined its parts into the other three provinces. But a president hadn't overseen the country for a few decades now. Megacorporations would never get together and agree on sharing a province with the provinces, theoretically losing one.

He scanned the empty pockets here and there among the populated areas. Those empty pockets represented the people in the country who would rather live in poverty than take the megacorporation's money to have all their likes and dislikes recorded for data collection. Johnny Ray couldn't wrap his head around those people. Not only would they be set for life financially, but, with the data that the implants transmitted, their lives would be enhanced and enriched.

The empty pockets devoid of orange dots denoting implants sometimes signified clusters of cyberpunks or freedom fighters. Most law-abiding citizens who refused the implants were few and far between, miles separating a single family—and the average family size was three. Cyberpunks were like the cattle of the ancients, herding together, thinking they had power in numbers. Foolish children were what they were, really.

Mr. Broad burst through Johnny Ray's office door, his assistant fumbling with his drink. "The reply from the abort message was that they were fleeing the subway."

"Oh, for Mother Dawn's sake," Johnny Ray cursed and jumped to his feet. "Lancelot?"

"Yes, sir."

"Is the drone still in flight?"

"It is conserving power atop the building, sir."

"Launch it right now to scan for the King of L.A. and the group of cyberpunks."

"Yes, sir."

The tele-skins now became a bird's-eye view of the pathways below. Both men scanned and spun as they frantically surveyed the tops of all the pedestrians' heads, searching for a cluster that included a man with white hair and a handful of teens.

The drone swooped and dove like a rollercoaster through side pathways, alleyways, parking lots. Then it shot upward to give the two men a more expansive view of the area.

Then Johnny Ray couldn't stop the smile from reaching ear to ear. It seemed Mother Dawn herself had handed success to him on a silver platter. And all he had to do was sit back and watch and reap the rewards.

He pointed to a building on the left tele-skin, where he spotted the unmistakable white-bearded man look behind himself one last time before disappearing through the front doors. Confident that the King of L.A. *and* the cyberpunks had taken refuge inside, Johnny Ray said, with a gleam in his eye, "Lancelot, deploy fifty slavebots to the Peppermint Lounge."

"What are their orders, sir?"

"Eliminate every human inside the building."

"Very good, sir."

"Program them to use the Brundle Teleporter. Let's be as stealthy as possible."

"Programming commencing now, sir. Target, the Peppermint Lounge and all its occupants."

A sense of accomplishment ran through Johnny Ray when his boss clasped a congratulatory hand on his shoulder and said, "Stellar work, partner."

"Sir?" Lancelot added. "The drone is critically low on battery. Permission to summon it back to the office to recharge?"

"Granted."

Johnny Ray rubbed his face as the morning sunlight breached his office windows and illuminated the room.

18

The sun crested the horizon, its rays accentuating all the orange dust that hung permanently in the air. Clawdy hefted her duffel bag to reposition it on her shoulder and to relieve some tension from the strap while she traversed the wide pathway between buildings. She had vague memories of living in a city when she had been a young girl, but she had spent so much of her teens and twenties in the commune that this landscape seemed foreign. Unpredictable. Dangerous. Maybe she shouldn't have left the protective bubble of the commune—as a thief on the run, to boot— and just tolerated the abuse.

But what had been done was done. She couldn't reverse time and change her desertion. She needed to move forward. Wherever *forward* might take her.

Small pockets of people slowly went from their homes to the pathway, adults on their way to work or children on their way to school. Clawdy fell in step with the pedestrians, no one paying her any mind. She turned the corner, and her mouth fell open. With eyes wide with wonder, she beheld the tallest building she had ever seen. Orange LED lights adorned the front awning that spelled CYBER-CORP.

Her heart hiccupped when she read the megacorporation's name. They were the ones who had invented and continued to infest Mother Dawn's creatures with the detestable Synchestria Implants. She didn't realize she had halted until a pedestrian, probably bustling to work, clipped her shoulder with his and almost sent her to the ground, the weight of her duffel bag knocking her off balance.

Clawdy steeled herself and let the strap fall off her shoulder to her wrist so the bag took a soft landing, not hitting the pavement at her feet. She had vials of trancing meds that she didn't dare waste. She scanned the pathway, now almost shoulder to shoulder with passersby, and wondered how many of these people had the Synchestria Implant.

How many had relinquished their integrity—their souls even—just to have the promise of financial stability? And yet Cyber-Corp still didn't pay enough, even while violating these people's bodies, for them to not have to work anymore. Yes, the payment was substantial, but it was not sustainable for the rest of their lives. A nice supplemental income, for sure, but worth allowing a megacorporation to record and to track all their senses?

Clawdy was sure Mother Dawn also did not approve.

Clawdy secured her strap on her shoulder again and turned from the Cyber-Corp skyscraper. Falling in line with the pedestrians, she matched their gait so she would not bump into anyone nor arise suspicion. Neuro-trancers didn't wear any special garb unless they were in a trancing session—like how she had heard the monks during the Age of Destruction had worn robes—but multiple customers had told her on numerous occasions that all neuro-trancers had a certain *look* to them that they couldn't quite put a finger on what. How neuro-trancers emitted some energy that commonfolk did not. And she was nervous about someone picking up on her energy out here in the great wide open, away from the commune. How would someone react to seeing a neuro-trancer in the wild?

Clawdy knew she had to find a good spot to hunker down, to collect herself, and to set up shop to begin taking customers. She would do it slowly, methodically, as to not panic the commoners. Little tidbits. Breadcrumbs and hints that a neuro-trancer was in the area. And open for business. Open to giving the tormented and the tortured a blessed pathway to Shangri-la.

After having this thought, Clawdy would have normally said *Praise Mother Dawn*, but the words got stuck in her throat, and, for the first time, she felt freed from the shackles of being a servant. She could still do Mother Dawn's bidding but now without the oppression and the servitude.

Clawdy realized she had just graduated to a higher level. The commune had been so restrictive. They waited for customers to come to them. Out here, she could be aggressive. Maybe she would be the start of a new dawn for the neuro-trancers. And she would be revered as the brave soul who broke from the archaic way of trancing and ushered in a new chapter in Mother Dawn's wishes.

She had been walking, head down, deep in thought and fantasy, and didn't notice the young man who had been matching her pace for the last two blocks. When she spotted him from the corner of her eye, she raised her head and regarded him. "Can I help you?" she asked in a mousy tone.

The young man scratched the back of his neck and broke eye contact but didn't change his pace, so they remained shoulder to shoulder. "My mother has a terminal illness."

Clawdy focused ahead. "I'm sorry to hear that."

"The disease will take a long time to kill her." He shot her a quick glance, then looked forward again. "She's in a lot of pain."

Clawdy wrung her hands together and bit a tiny scab off her bottom lip. She wondered how this stranger had identified her so quickly. Were the goggles sitting atop her forehead enough of a clue to tip him off? Or maybe this was a ruse. They'd had a few instances of anti-Mother Dawn fanatics who had tried to infiltrate the commune to destroy all the work the neuro-trancers do there. Was this young man one of those? If she acknowledged what he was implying, would he immediately shank her, leaving her to bleed out on the side of the pathway?

But she realized she would be no good to anyone if she lived in constant fear. She knew this was the chance she would have to take when she had fled the safety of the commune.

"Does she want to be hypnotized?" Clawdy murmured.

The young man grabbed her wrist, and her heart hammered, exploding adrenaline through her veins. "I knew you were one of the chosen. I could … feel it radiating from you."

Clawdy's heart rate tried to settle, now with the threat being nonexistent. "Does she want this, or is this you wanting it for her? I can't let anyone go through the trancing if they don't want it themselves. That would curse both her soul on the other side, as well as yours, for eternity."

The young man nodded. "She's too sick to make the trip to the complex. In too much pain."

Clawdy recognized, with that statement, just how many people may be suffering and couldn't get to the commune for help. How many people could the neuro-trancers relieve of their pain and send to Shangri-la if they could just leave their blasted land?

A grin formed on her lips. She truly was now a savior among the streets. "Please take me to her."

17

Adam was exhausted—physically, mentally, emotionally, spiritually—but that didn't keep him from staying awake a bit longer in the haven of the lounge. He laid on the cot, Venus to his right, Jonesy to his left, all deep in slumber, along with Cherie and Mony and a few dozen adult strangers who he didn't know why they were here or what their purpose was in the lounge. He was confident they were safe. He should despise the assassin for killing Maggie, but the man had risked his own life to get them out of the subway and brought them to a place that seemed to be a larger operation of what Adam's band of cyberpunks had been trying to accomplish.

Adam kept one eye closed but used the opened one to scan the large warehouse-like space. He spotted the assassin in what looked like a heated discussion with the barkeep. Both were using their hands to punctuate whatever points they were trying to make. Then the assassin pointed to Adam while in conversation, and Adam closed his opened eye so they wouldn't know he was spying on them.

He waited a few beats before opening one eye again. Both men were standing, silent, and focused on the passageway that separated the front bar area from this warehouse section. Adam's heart jumped, and he opened both eyes. Something wasn't right. Did they hear something out there?

Adam watched the assassin creep toward the closed door that led to the passageway. The barkeep remained standing in place, and the assassin now had his clipper in his hands. Adam sat upright in his cot, focused on the door.

The assassin noticed Adam's movements and gave him the signal to be quiet but to wake the others. Adam leaned across the space between the cots and gently rubbed Venus's arm. "Hey, babe. Wake up, but be quiet," he whispered.

"*Hrm?* What's happening?"

Adam put a finger to his lips and pointed to the assassin. Venus nodded in understanding and turned to wake Cherie while Adam worked on Jonesy. Once all five cyberpunks were awake and standing at the foot of their cots, Adam cleared his throat to get the assassin's attention. He pointed to the other handful of sleeping strangers and shrugged, indicating that he needed to know if he should wake them too.

The assassin nodded, then trained his attention back to the door as he approached it.

The cyberpunks spread out and gently woke all the sleeping adults. Like a wave in the ocean, each awoke in turn, and within seconds, all occupants of the lounge were awake and on high alert.

Adam watched the assassin put his ear to the door. Adam couldn't hear anything from where he stood, but he assumed the assassin had heard something unsettling. Adam glanced at the barkeep again, who stood ramrod straight and now had his own weapon in hand. And it wasn't a clipper. It was something Adam had never seen before.

The assassin moving away from the door and shaking his head made Adam refocus on the door. He felt Venus slip her hand into his, interlacing their fingers. He could tell she was scared; he knew they all were. It was one thing to plan for attacks and to pilfer empty railway cars, but it was totally different when clipper rounds were flying over their heads and the enemy was in front of them. He squeezed her hand in reassurance, and, with her free hand, she gripped the inside of his forearm, either as a sign of affection or as additional protection; he wasn't sure which.

The assassin walked backward, keeping his focus on the door, and spun a finger in the air. Adam wasn't quite sure what that symbolized, but the barkeep spun on his heels, made the same motion in the air, and all the adults in the room turned and started in the same direction—toward the rear of the warehouse area they were in.

Adam scanned his friends' faces, mimicked the finger-spin motion, and turned to lead them with others toward the same spot. He assumed the building must have a multitude of hidden passageways and secret exits for escape. These people seemed to know what they were doing. Or at least have a contingency plan for any—

The door to the passageway that led into the bar area behind them blew completely off its hinges in a cloud of smoke and dust. Adam landed on the floor and threw his body atop Venus's for protection until he ascertained what had just happened. Then clipper rounds filled the room, coming from the doorway.

Adam turned to look behind them, as many of the adults had already gotten to their feet and sprinted toward the far back exit. Adam's eyes widened, and his jaw dropped when he saw robotic machines that walked on two legs and had arms and a head resembling a human—unlike any robots he had ever seen in his life before, which traveled on wheels and were box-shaped.

The machines cascaded through the doorway, two at a time, and with each entrance, the robot unloaded their clipper.

"Are they people in protective gear?" the barkeep yelled, firing his weapon at the doorway as he ran.

Adam grabbed Venus under her arms to lift her to her feet and thought the barkeep's guess made sense. Maybe these were soldiers.

"I don't think so!" the assassin yelled over the chaos, ducking and weaving toward the back door.

Adam pushed Venus to get her moving, and a clipper round struck one of the adults as they tried to run past Adam. They collapsed to the floor, eyes still open, the left side of their brain oozing like goo from the gaping hole.

"Go, go, go!" Adam yelled to his whole crew.

Jonesy and Cherie ran hunched over, and Mony collided with one of the adults when she took her first step, the force sprawling her out on the floor.

Adam glanced behind him. At least ten of those robots had entered the room and were advancing. He pushed Venus a little harder and checked to ensure Mony had gotten to her feet. In that brief time, he watched clipper rounds strike four more adults. The cots exploded into the air from the impact when the rounds hit them. Hundreds of rounds found their mark in the warehouse area, with pieces of the wall and ceiling creating dust plumes.

Someone screamed behind Adam, and he turned in a panic. It sounded like Cherie's voice, but it was just another young woman, whose nose and mouth were completely missing from where the round had hit.

The first handful of adults had reached the back door and were scrambling through. Adam noticed the assassin was not firing back at the robots but maintained a weaving path for Adam. Why was the man heading toward him and not the exit door to safety?

More robots entered through the passageway door, which meant more clipper rounds filled the air. That also meant Adam watched the robots pick off more of the fleeing horde, and they dropped, usually whole parts of their body now a cavernous hole.

The assassin reached Adam, threw an arm around his shoulders, and used his own body as a shield and a force to make them go faster. Adam still had his hands on Venus's back to keep her pace from slowing.

"Why aren't you firing back?" Adam had to scream for the assassin to hear him over the discharge of the robot's clippers.

"Only have a dozen or so rounds left. Gotta last me until I can recharge!"

Adam's stomach churned. That was not a good sign. They had a world-elite assassin and freedom fighter now helping them, and the man can't even use his weapon to protect them.

Adam heard Cherie scream, then Venus screamed and spun away from his guiding hands to land on the floor next to her fallen friend.

The assassin growled in his ear, "Keep moving."

Adam bucked to try to free himself from the man's grasp, but it was too tight. He looked over his shoulder to see Venus on her knees, tears streaking her face, as she placed her hands on Cherie's chest. Their friend's face was missing, from her nose upward. Just gone. Brain matter and blood covered the floor where she had landed.

Adam jerked again, this time with more adrenaline and anger, but the assassin's grip tightened.

"I said to keep moving. She's dead."

"No, you prick. Venus!"

The assassin glanced behind them at Venus, now draped over her friend's desecrated body.

"I'm not leaving her!"

The assassin gripped Adam behind his neck, bent him forward, and grabbed his forearm to keep him moving and to remove any leverage the teen might have to break free. "She is not the important one."

"She's important to me!"

"And you're important to me. Keep moving."

"Venus!" Adam yelled, turning his head to look behind him. "You gotta keep moving! Jonesy, go grab Venus and make her move!"

Jonesy nodded and spun from the horde to return to where Venus lay sprawled across her friend.

Clipper rounds struck the floor right at their feet. Adam felt the tiny concussion blasts against his legs when they hit the orange concrete. He had to jump over a few dead adults in his path who didn't make it out. But he saw the bottleneck grew smaller, as most of the people who had been in the warehouse area now were outside. He turned back to look at Jonesy practically yanking Venus along. At least they were traveling in the right direction.

Adam looked at the robots, who had made it halfway across the area themselves, still advancing, still firing. Still picking off escaping people here and there. He was certain that, if just a handful more of those machines had arrived, none of the people in that room would have survived.

The assassin was ready to push Adam through the exit door to safety, so Adam turned and screamed at Jonesy and Venus, "Just get outside, and I'll find you! Watch out for those rounds!"

"Where's Mony?" Jonesy yelled back.

"I hope outside already," was all Adam could get out before the assassin shoved him through the doorway to freedom. Chunks of wall and ceiling fell on his head and shoulders from clipper rounds blanketing the doorway. Yet he stumbled into the outside world, the assassin still pushing him.

"Now we run," the man said and quickened his pace.

Adam looked behind him, waiting for Venus and Jonesy to come through the doorway. He counted in his head how many steps they were behind him and converted it into how many seconds it should take for them to break free. He spotted Mony running with one of the small surviving groups of adults, relieved that at least he hadn't lost that friend too. He refocused on the door, growing farther away as his legs now carried him at full a sprint.

The seconds it should have taken for Venus and Jonesy to escape had far surpassed. Neither his best friend nor his girlfriend had come through the door.

Johnny Ray sipped on his glass of orange liquor while he watched the invasion on his 360-degree tele-skin, from the slavebots' vantage. Each had a camera built into its head, and Johnny Ray could switch between which unit he wanted to see the perspective from. Heck, he could activate all their cameras and have the tele-skin break up into multiple mini screens. But he found more enjoyment having one large view of the attack and the eradication of the enemy.

Through the smoke and dust of concrete and plaster from the initial wave of the bot invasion, Johnny Ray spotted a multitude of bodies on the floor, motionless. Then he discerned all the blood and limbs scattered to and fro. A smile crept upon his lips as increased screams penetrated his office.

In the distance, he saw the rear door open and watched small pockets of people escape. That was okay. If a few fish escaped the nets, it meant the fishermen were handling most of them. He sipped the orange liquid again, letting it burn and soothe his throat. Then he recognized the King of L.A. He had one of the cyberpunks in a death grip, leading him toward the door—one of the punks that Cyber-Corp had hired the assassin to kill. Johnny Ray needed no more confirmation than what he just saw. Traitor.

Toward the left side, he spotted another cyberpunk kneeling over what looked like a dead one. Johnny Ray switched cameras to use a bot positioned more on that side of the room so that the kids were now in the center of the screen. He smiled when he realized that the female on her knees was a sitting duck. Then he saw another boy turn and run back to her. Intrigued to see how this would play out, Johnny Ray sat back and took another sip.

He watched the boy grab the girl and force her to head toward the door. Johnny Ray adjusted his view to the door and saw that the King of L.A. had gotten the boy he was pushing through. What was so special about that boy? Johnny Ray would have to brief Mr. Broad on that.

He rechecked the girl and her friend running, now side by side, toward the exit. They were part of the cyberpunk cell with the boy who had gained the King of L.A.'s attention. Now Johnny Ray knew how he would figure out what was so special about that boy—a boy that the King of L.A. would risk his own life to save.

All too easy.

"Lancelot."

"Yes, sir."

"Tell the slavebots to cease fire. Do not kill the two remaining humans but capture them before they reach the exit."

"Very good, sir."

His tele-skin showed the bots throwing clipper rounds at the two running teens. Then all weapons silenced.

And from the right side of the camera angle, a bot moved like lightning across the floor and scooped up both teens in its arms. Johnny Ray heard the clicking noise of the locks securing, turning its arms into a mini jail.

"Capture times two successful, sir."

Johnny Ray watched the teen girl frantically try to pull the bot's arms apart to escape. He chuckled at her futile attempts. "Thank you, Lancelot. Have the bot bring them to my office. The rest of the militia can return to their charging pods."

"Very good, sir."

Johnny Ray clicked off his tele-skin and took a long swallow to finish the drink. All he had to do now was wait for the bot to arrive with the two cyberpunks, and he would get all the answers he needed about that *special* boy.

21

The young man knocked on his mother's bedroom door, Clawdy standing behind him. "Maw-maw?"

"Come in, come in," Clawdy heard the weak and frail voice answer.

He pushed open the door to expose a musty and dim room. A dresser sat against a wall underneath a single window, and a bed lay in the middle of the room, occupied by a lump, which Clawdy assumed was a human being.

"I brought someone who might help you," the young man said and stepped aside.

"Oh?" The blankets rustled, and a cough emanated from the bed, then the woman's head appeared.

Clawdy thought she looked older than her probably thirtysomething age and smelled death not too far off. The woman was racked with coughs again, and Clawdy heard the death rattle in the woman's lungs. The woman's face scrunched in what seemed to be excruciating pain.

Clawdy set her bagful of trancing serum and syringes gently on the floor and approached the bedside.

The woman smiled and reached a shaky hand, then held it in midair, waiting for Clawdy to take it. "You look like an angel."

"Far from it, ma'am." Clawdy flashed the woman the warmest smile she could muster.

"She's a neuro-trancer, Maw-maw."

The woman's eyebrows raised. "A neuro-trancer? Out here in the city? I didn't know you made house calls now."

Clawdy kept the smile on her face to ease the woman's doubts. "I was passing through, and your son recognized me. I did not plan to do any trancing today, but a neuro-trancer is never off duty, as we say."

"Praise Mother Dawn," the woman barely sputtered.

"Mother Dawn be praised," the son replied from behind them.

Clawdy chose not to add the appropriate response and hoped neither would notice. She laid a loving hand on the woman's arm to comfort her. "We are obligated to ask you if you want to be hypnotized, and you must reply verbally in order for us to continue."

"I thought it was called trancing?" the son asked, stepping to the opposite side of the bed so he could hold his mother's other hand. "What's hypnotizing?"

"*Trancing* describes the state of your being when it has crossed over to Shangri-la. *Hypnotized* is the act of a neuro-trancer injecting the trancing serum into you."

"Then why not just ask if they want to enter a state of trancing?"

Clawdy sighed. In all her years of trancing, no one had ever asked this question. But then again, she had never made a house call outside the commune. "Because Mother Dawn mandates it. It was part of the instructions she gave the elders, when they all heard her speak to them in tones." She flinched internally, thinking of Cain and how he had claimed to have also heard those same tones.

"Praise Mother Dawn," the son replied.

Clawdy met the woman's gaze. "Ma'am, do you want to be hypnotized?"

The woman eyed her son, maybe looking for an answer, maybe looking for confidence or permission, whatever, but when another round of hacking shook her body and left her winded, she nodded. "Yes. Yes, I do." She laid her hand over her son's hand. "I will miss you over there. And I love you."

"This is the right thing, Maw-maw."

Clawdy opened her bag, removed a syringe and a vial of trancing serum, filled the needle, and turned to the woman. "We usually have a heart monitor hooked up to tell us when you've finally entered paradise, but we'll have to wing it here. Is that still okay?"

"Oh dear, I'm sure you'll know when I have crossed over. You won't hear these tired old lungs gasping for air anymore."

Clawdy nodded. "Fair enough." She looked at the son. "Did you want to be here for it?"

"Absolutely."

Clawdy smiled at the woman and pushed the tip of the needle through her skin. She had done this so many times that she didn't even need to watch the insertion. She pushed the plunger, and before five ticks of the clock had gone by, the woman's eyes closed. And her chest no longer heaved for breath.

"Thank you," the son murmured. "What do we do now? With her body?"

Clawdy's eyes widened. She hadn't thought of that. On the commune, they had a large incinerator where they cremated the bodies at the end of every week. What in Mother Dawn's name did Clawdy do with the bodies out here, in the middle of the city?

Thinking quickly, she asked, "Did your mother have a favorite place to visit? Or a childhood memory of a location that was dear to her?" She paused and contemplated whether what she would suggest next might sound distasteful, but she decided to offer it anyway. "Or, since you know that she was terminal, you could call the authorities and have them take her, as if she had passed naturally."

The son fell into deep thought. Just when Clawdy was about to say something else to break the heavy silence, he replied, "The lake. She would tell me stories about fishing on the lake, in a rowboat, when she was a girl with my grandfather."

"I think that would suit her just perfectly." Clawdy placed a delicate hand on the son's arm for encouragement. "Do you have a way to get her out there, or do you need my help?"

He shook his head. "I want to do it. It's my last goodbye."

Clawdy patted his arm and headed for the door.

"What do I owe you?" he asked, making her stop.

She had been so wrapped up in the steps of the illegal trancing that she had forgotten about payment. She hadn't considered what her price would be yet; a normal fee would be the entirety of the customer's assets and credits, deposited into a mutual account to honor Mother Dawn. Clawdy assumed she would have more time to come up with her fee. She didn't even know she had said it, until she heard her voice say, "This one's on the house."

"Thank you, ma'am."

She smirked, but it wasn't completely full of pleasure. "Praise Mother Dawn."

"Mother Dawn be praised," he appropriately responded.

She closed the door behind her, now wondering where all the money they collected from customers actually went. And who was in charge of the funds?

22

The King of L.A. grabbed Adam's shoulder, just as he realized the boy was about to turn back toward the lounge.

Adam violently shrugged the assassin's hand off him. "I gotta go back for them!" He tried to break into a sprint, but the King of L.A. tackled Adam, the man's two large arms bringing Adam to the ground from behind.

The King of L.A.'s breath was against Adam's ear as they lay on the ground. "You won't do anyone any good if you die now. You don't even know if they are still alive."

Adam let the weight of the man keep him pinned as he collected his thoughts and stared at the open door in the distance. "There's no more shooting."

"Exactly. So, either your friends are dead or they escaped another way. I highly doubt they are still in there and alive, so going back is suicide."

Adam adjusted his arm and pushed so the assassin would get the hint to get off him. When the King of L.A. stood, Adam saw Mony approaching them.

She proffered a hand to help him get to his feet. "Where are the others?"

Adam brushed orange dirt off his pants, then clapped a few times to get it off his hands. "Cheri was hit, so Venus ran to her and refused to leave her. So Jonesy went back for Venus. They didn't come out."

Mony's face tightened, and her hands balled into fists. "Then we have to go back and find them."

Adam regarded the assassin, signaling that the man should explain why they weren't, that way Adam wouldn't appear heartless to his friend.

"No one goes back in there," the assassin said and pushed past the two teens, clipping Mony's shoulder with his own.

"What's going on?" she whispered as they headed in the same direction as the small pockets of people who had escaped alive.

Adam grumbled, "I hate to say it, but he's right. They either didn't make it out, or they got out some other way."

"What other way, Adam?" she almost growled. "If there was another way, then I'm sure all of us would have scattered. The fact that every single person in there tried to get through the same door should tell you how many ways there were to leave."

"What about back through the front door of the lounge itself?" He glanced at her, searching for some sign of hope in her expression. He just wasn't ready to admit that he may have lost his girlfriend and his best friend all in the same few minutes.

As they walked, Mony kicked a rock and watched it skip and skirt in the dirt away from them. "So, you think they went *toward* the bots and what? Under their legs and through the lounge?" They walked in silence for a moment, until she added, "You saw how many people those things killed. They were picking them off like flies. It's a wonder that even the two of *us* got out."

Adam scrunched his face and shot daggers at her from his eyes. "Are you saying you believe they are dead? Just like that?"

"What makes them special, Adam? More special than all those other people who died in there? Because *you* cared about them? You don't think all these people"—she waved her arm to indicate the few pockets of people meandering across the field—"also had friends or family in there who were killed? Just because it was Venus and Jonesy doesn't mean they had any more chance to live."

Adam felt a sensation like fire mixed with ice in his stomach. What Mony had said wasn't untrue, but he still wanted to believe his friends were special. And maybe had survived.

Adam quickened his pace to catch up to the assassin. "Where are we headed?"

"Somewhere to hide and to regroup. And to come up with a plan."

"I assumed that. But *where*?"

The assassin sniffed quickly and rubbed his nose with his sleeve, then ran his hand through his white beard. "The wastelands."

"No way Venus or Jonesy will find us out there if they got out," Adam said frantically.

"You need to give that a rest," the assassin said. "We must focus on the task at hand."

"What *is* your allegiance?" Mony asked. "I feel we have quickly forgotten that you killed Maggie, and now we're listening to you like you're the leader of us now." She scowled and looked at Adam. "C'mon. Let's go back. We've always been on our own, survived on our own. As soon as this jerk came into our life, we went from six strong to just the two of us. It's not a coincidence."

The assassin spun on his heel and halted, kicking up orange dust. "If it weren't for me, you would all be dead. And I refuse to take credit for the three we lost in the lounge. I've never seen bots like that before."

"But you brought us to that lounge as a haven," she growled and stepped closer to the man.

"Just stop," Adam murmured. "We knew the risk when we went off the grid."

"The megacorporations will always hunt cyberpunks," the assassin said. "Whether it's employing people like me or deploying machines to find and kill you."

"I don't understand why you're helping us now. If you are part of these … freedom fighters, then why would you let Cyber-Corp hire you to kill us?" Adam asked.

The assassin started walking again. He pulled a pair of binocular glasses from his orange leather jacket and secured them onto his nose. His head swiveled as he said, "Looks clear. The wastelands are in a few more miles." He stowed his glasses in his pocket.

"Why are the corporations still hiring the same person who is also killing their own people?" Mony asked.

"They don't know it's me. I've never failed on a hit. And always with no witnesses. They have no idea the person they are hiring for a job may have just killed their assistant the day before. Plus I'm not the only one in the business, as you saw earlier in the subway."

Adam scratched his head while paying attention to the uneven ground beneath his feet as he walked. "Why hasn't anyone just paid you or the other assassins to kill the CEO of Cyber-Corp, and all of this would be over."

Mony chuckled. "Because they would have a new CEO before he even left the building."

"Precisely," the assassin said. "When I get hired to hit someone in the megacorporations, it's usually something personal." He stopped and donned his binocular glasses again, scanning. "We'll get there tomorrow. Need to camp for the night." He pointed southwest.

Adam followed the man's finger with his gaze, and all he could see was endless miles and miles of orange desert, all the way to the horizon. "Where is *there*?"

"Where we will be safest." The assassin patted Adam's shoulder and bustled forward again.

Adam shot Mony a look, as if to say, *I hope this guy isn't crazy*. He glanced around to see that the small pockets of people hadn't broken from their clusters but hadn't slowed their pace, also toward the same indistinct point in the distance. He noticed for the first time that the Peppermint Lounge barkeep was among the ranks.

Adam squinted to see if maybe he could see something he wasn't seeing, but all he saw was the wastelands: the most barren area in the West Coast Province, where no one would dare tread—not even the megacorporations—because the heat and the sun would kill anyone, if the wildlife didn't.

He reached for Mony's hand, and she squeezed. "Venus and Jonesy will never think to check the wastelands for us."

Mony nodded. "Then we'll have to go look for them." She checked to see how far they were from eavesdroppers. "We can skedaddle when everyone's asleep. Go back to the city."

Adam smiled for the first time in what felt like forever.

23

The unharmed Chameleon twin pushed through Johnny Ray's office door without knocking, determined to get answers as to why Cyber-Corp had aborted their mission. And to ensure that didn't mean they weren't going to pay him and his brother either.

He saw the backs of Johnny Ray's and Mr. Broad's heads before each man turned to face him. The twin stopped and, unprompted, said, "In case you're wondering, my brother is fine. Lost an ear. Just a flesh wound. He's back at the house, recouping."

Mr. Broad clasped an orange remote control in his hands and slowly came around the table in the center of the room. "That is fantastic news. I'm sure you're wondering why we called you off mid mission."

"I don't care about that as much as getting the payment we agreed upon. In full."

"You shall have your money, possibly more."

The twin raised an eyebrow.

"That's if you're willing to alter the current mission."

"I'm listening."

Mr. Broad waggled his fingers to signal for the twin to stand alongside Johnny Ray, who was studying something the twin couldn't see.

As the twin approached, the two virtuality cages came into view. And inside each was a teenager, a boy and a girl—

two of the cyberpunks from the subway. He had an urge to wind up and kick the two boxes for the trouble the punks had given him on the platform, but he knew his foot would just bounce off the orange pulsing lights that comprise the cage—lights stronger than steel and used to only contain the most-hardened criminals and politicians. He felt some satisfaction that these two deviants were imprisoned in the same boxes that the most wretched and vile scum called home until they died.

The girl had her knees brought to her chin, her arms over her legs, her forehead resting on her forearm, her hair covering her face. She made no motion to acknowledge that another person had entered the room. The boy sat upright, reclined backward on his hands, a smug look plastered on his face. The twin assassin wanted to smash through the virtuality lights and send the punk's teeth flying with one swing.

"We received intel that a major cell of cyberpunks were using the warehouse attached to the Peppermint Lounge as a war room of sorts," Mr. Broad said—cool, calm, and collected—without looking at the twin. We dispatched a squad of slavebots to clean out the infestation, and the cats brought home some mice."

The boy spat a wad of spittle, and it sizzled when it hit the virtuality light bars. The twin chuckled at the kid's poor excuse for an insult.

"We wanted you to get a good look at their faces," Johnny Ray said. "We have bigger plans for them."

The twin rubbed his chin and nodded toward Jonesy. "I won't forget that pretty one's face, but the girl needs to lift her head."

"Hey, sweet cheeks," Johnny Ray said, "lift that pretty little face of yours so our friend here can get a really *good* look."

Venus didn't raise her head but muttered something into her arms.

"I'm sorry. Maybe you didn't hear me. Lift that pretty face of yours."

Again something that sounded like a two-word expletive came from under the curtain of orange hair.

"Venus, don't listen to them," Jonesy said from his virtuality cage.

Without warning, Mr. Broad pressed a button on the orange remote in his hand, and Jonesy's body arched backward, every muscle rigid, his eyes bulging from his skull, white foam pluming from his mouth—then his body collapsed onto the floor of the cage. He lay panting, curled into the fetal position.

Mr. Broad focused on Venus. "My assistant instructed you to show your face."

A smile spread from ear to ear on the twin's face when he saw Mr. Broad's finger twitch over the button that would electrocute the brat in her cage. He almost hoped she wouldn't obey, just so he could see the currents bend her body to almost breaking in half.

Venus never moved her head.

Mr. Broad pushed the button, and the cyberpunk's body arched like a cat, her hair like a waterfall pulsing from the electricity, her eyes almost popping from their sockets, a scream caught in her throat that turned guttural—inhuman almost. Then she landed like a dead fish, all her muscles gooey and incapacitated.

"Take them away and stow them in the security bunker," Mr. Broad instructed two slavebots in the corner. The bots came to life, stalked toward the two virtuality cages, lifted them from the handles on the tops, and marched from the office with the two recovering teens.

"What's the plan, boss?" the twin asked, pouring himself a complimentary drink from the side table.

"We are going to release them."

The twin paused mid sip to ensure he had heard the man correctly.

"The King of L.A. was with them, very attentive to helping a certain boy escape."

"He helped the whole lot of them escape in the subway."

"This boy is different," Johnny Ray interjected. "I watched in first POV from the bot cameras, and the King of L.A. favored this boy over all the others. Even let some die, just so he could get this boy to safety. Does that sound like his MO?"

The twin tilted his head in disbelief. "Not for that prick. That's way off base."

"Right," Mr. Broad continued. "We'll install Synchestria Implants into these two kids so we can track them back to their den. Back to the King of L.A. and, more important, back to the *special* boy so we can see what's so exceptional about him."

The twin waggled a finger with the hand that held the glass. "Bait. I like it. Let them do the hard work for me. My brother will be mended by then too. Double the fun."

Johnny Ray added, "We'll need you to follow them but discreetly. Only to ensure they don't try to find a 3-11 Eleven Man to have the implants removed before they go back to their friends. You'll have to persuade them to change their mind, if that becomes their plan."

The twin scratched his orange beard. "Why these extra steps? Wouldn't it be faster and less complicated if you just hand them over to me and my brother, and we *persuade* them to bring us to their camp? And then let us wipe them all outright then and there? One-stop shopping. In and out."

Johnny Ray snickered, and Mr. Broad raised a hand to get him to quit it. He stoically regarded the Chameleon twin. "You are a tad bit overconfident in your abilities. While you and your brother no doubt have proven to now be the elite among assassins, do you really think you have the expertise to wipe out a cell of freedom fighters, who already feel like they have nothing to lose? Just the two of you? And remember. The King of L.A. has now exposed that he's a traitor, that he has always sided with them. He alone will give you a run for your credits."

The twin pursed his lips, looking like he wanted to rebut but also like he accepted how that plan would be disastrous for his brother and him.

"Let our slavebots do the dirty work," Johnny Ray added. "You just ensure the two captives, upon their release, don't try to remove the implants. So when they reunite with their little pack, the slavebots will spray the area with clipper rounds."

"Because that worked so well last time," the twin muttered.

"I do not need to justify my decisions to the hired help," Mr. Broad growled, "but, if you didn't notice, there are far, far less of them than there were originally in the lounge. We cut their numbers by 70 percent. I have full faith that my bots can eradicate the remainder." Mr. Broad set the virtuality cage remote on his desk and glared at the twin. "And, once our two new friends find their comrades, and the bots have killed them all, you will only have one directive. Bring the *special* boy to me, alive."

011000011111000111011100

Johnny Ray was on his second drink, comfortably sitting on his orange couch in his office, replaying the day's events through his mind and basking in the images of Mr. Broad electrocuting those two cyberpunks. He knew watching the technicians install, into their heads, the one piece of technology that these cyberpunks were fighting against would feel like some vindication for all the hardships the teens had caused Cyber-Corp throughout the years. Not just this particular group but the teens who were now adults somewhere. Cyberpunks had been trying to take down Cyber-Corp for years, and now the megacorporation will send these deviants into the wild, tainted with the technology that will help finally destroy their little rebellion.

He took a sip, smirking at the karma, when his door flung open, and his boss stalked into the office. Some liquid in the glass splashed onto his orange shirt when he rose too quickly, startled.

"I need to show you something," was all Mr. Broad said and stormed down the hallway toward his office.

Johnny Ray sighed, hoping whatever it was wouldn't diminish the high he felt from capturing the two brats, and followed his boss into the office.

Mr. Broad said, "Lancelot."

"Yes, sir."

"Replay today's Synchestria anomaly."

Johnny Ray raised an eyebrow at his boss.

Mr. Broad pointed to the tele-skin to redirect Johnny Ray's attention.

Cyber-Corp tasked Lancelot—well, a *lot* of Lancelots—with constantly uploading all the data received from everyone who had a Synchestria Implant into the mainframe. The programs dissected the five senses of the implant carrier, and whenever a loyal customer liked or disliked something that should not be there, the mainframe would mark it as an anomaly and would report it to Mr. Broad.

Johnny Ray leaned his head forward, saw something, but didn't move. He squinted to try to change what was playing out on the monitor. Because there was no way this could be happening. Had their own creed of what kept them glued to Mother Dawn come undone?

"A modification?" Even saying it aloud still didn't make it feel real. "Is that possible?"

They watched the image on the screen until Mr. Broad paused the replay at the exact moment where they could see it clearest. "That drunkard in the Peppermint Lounge's *Like* meter went off the chain when he saw the boy's eyes, after the boy entered the bar with the King of L.A. Almost crashed the mainframe."

Johnny Ray ran a finger through his eyebrow in rising anxiety. "Do you think more than one is roaming around? Or is this boy a singular event?"

"It's the only anomaly today, so hopefully he's the only one. But they could be out there in packs right now, for all we know."

"Just having one confirmed is … bad enough."

Mr. Broad smacked his lips. "You're tellin' me."

"We would lose everything if the neuro-trancers found out about him, if they learned the truth. It would expose us."

Mr. Broad shot Johnny Ray a side-eye and slammed his palms onto his desk, the sound reverberating through his office. In a growl, he spat, "And that's why you'll ensure every neuro-trancer is wiped out. By all means necessary."

Johnny Ray let a moment pass before adding to the conundrum, allowing his boss to calm a bit before he reminded Mr. Broad of the financial issue of killing all the neuro-trancers. "Sir. If we get rid of the neuro-trancers, we would lose one quarter of our annual income. Is that … wise?"

Mr. Broad ran a finger across his right eyebrow and smacked his lips. "Do you think the long-term success of this company resides in how we collect all the trancing money from them, or does it rest on the shoulders of ensuring they never learn about the blue-eyed boy? Because that would pull the plug on Cyber-Corp. Forever."

Johnny Ray didn't need to respond. He knew the answer. Losing one quarter of their assets was a small price to pay for the overall survival of the company, like amputating an arm to save the body. And it was time to sever that limb.

Clawdy kept her head low as she scurried through the pathways—*roads*, she thought the ancients had called them. They had originally used these *roads* when they had mechanical transportation that rolled on wheels. But now, during the current Age of Oblivion, these weather-worn *roads* were walking paths, since the Brundle Teleporters had replaced those wheeled vehicles eons ago, for those who *could* even afford Brundle Teleporter access.

She spied the small huts and bungalows lining the pathways—no one lived in any structure larger than a few rooms—and the skyscraping behemoths in the distance, each home to another megacorporation, each playing a part in the reason why governments had dissolved and why power had been handed to the businesses.

Because, in the Age of Oblivion, didn't the corporations know better what the people needed and wanted? This wasn't the Age of Destruction anymore, where governments and municipalities had the citizens' best interests at heart. In this era, commerce knew exactly how to make the citizens' lives content and happy.

All thanks to the breakthrough technology of Cyber-Corp's Synchestria Implants.

And just the thought of the megacorporation's name nauseated Clawdy—especially when she imagined all these millions of people going through life and having a company spy and record everything the citizens do. She wondered if the ancients ever had to worry about atrocities like these.

She snapped herself from her internal ramblings and realized she needed shelter—somewhere to hunker down, until she could get her bearings and could find something permanent. She would have to take payments for trancing from here on out. That freebie earlier today couldn't become the norm—otherwise she wouldn't have any funds to live on.

Clawdy pulled her hood to her orange jacket over her head to shield her eyes from the blustery wind blowing orange dust across the pathways. She shuffled with the other pedestrians, eyeing signs to spot somewhere to crash for the night.

She stopped at an intersection and read the flashing orange neon sign in the window. PEPPERMINT LOUNGE. She rubbed her hands together and smacked her lips. She hadn't realized how parched she was, until she considered drinking a nice cool glass of clean water. And this place seemed like just the place to quench her thirst.

Clawdy opened the front door of the lounge and stepped inside.

25

"This is a good place to camp for the night," Adam heard the one-eyed assassin say, taking the role of migration leader for the small pockets of rebels who comprised their makeshift convoy into the wastelands.

Adam watched the people, their faces haggard and dirty and downtrodden, plop themselves onto the orange desert floor. Some faces remained tear stained from losing a friend or loved one during the Peppermint Lounge massacre. Adam watched the barkeep place the back of his hand against his forehead and sigh heavily.

Adam used only his eyes to try to get a headcount, then collapsed onto the ground next to Mony. "Only about thirty of us are here. How many do you think those robots killed?"

Mony rubbed her eyes with her palms, probably to flush out the dust. "At least one hundred of us were in the back room."

Adam fell silent and sighed, looking across the barren landscape.

"You holding up okay?" she asked.

He nodded, then glanced at her with his ice-blue eyes. "I really want Venus and Jonesy to be alive. At first, I wanted them to be alive *and* healthy. At this point, I'll be happy with alive and hurt, because at least we can get them help."

The assassin dropped into a cross-legged sitting position next to the two teens, creating a small circle of three. "We have a few more miles to walk tomorrow to reach our destination. Once we arrive, they will take care of all your needs—clothes, food, water, beds … showers."

"You still haven't told us what this place is," Adam said, playing with a pebble he had picked up from the ground.

"The most secret place in the country. Beyond the reaches of tracking from those who don't know it exists."

Adam shot Mony a look. "And why are you taking us there?"

The assassin stroked his white beard, then reclined on his palms. "Not *us*. You. You are the prize."

Adam rose to his feet and put his hands on his waist. "Prize of *what*? Why do you talk in freaking riddles all the time?"

The assassin tugged on Adam's orange shirt to get him to sit, then chuckled. "Cool your jets, before you blow a fuse. All in due time. Everything in steps. First step is to reach our destination without anyone falling out from exhaustion or heat stroke tomorrow."

Mony squinted to scrutinize the assassin's silver foxlike appearance. "How old are you?"

The man shook his head, laughing. "Why do you care?"

"I've never seen anyone with white hair. That was the color of the ancients when they aged beyond a certain birthdate."

The assassin nodded toward Adam and smiled warmly. "And have you ever seen another human being with blue eyes? Have you given him the third degree about his eye color?"

"My eyes didn't change color though," Adam countered. "I was born like this."

"*Ahh*. How do you know my hair changed color? Maybe I was born like this too."

"I don't buy it," Mony said. "You still have gray hair mixed in with the white. You are aging. That is different."

The assassin laughed and wiped his palms on his orange pants to clean off the desert dust. "I like your attention to detail. It might save your life one day. During the Age of Destruction, the ancients would consider it disrespectful to ask someone their age. But I will tell you that you are correct about me living well past the life expectancy in the Age of Oblivion."

"And being an assassin for the evil entities as well as a freedom fighter against those same entities too? That's like a triple win," Adam said.

The man grunted as he stood, his aging muscles and joints not cooperating as easily as they did in his youth. "We need some shut-eye. Tomorrow will be a few more hours of trekking to get to where we're going."

Mony shot Adam a knowing look; the time to break from the group and head back to the city was coming.

The assassin reached into his jacket and removed a pair of orange wrist fetters. "Can't afford for the prize to dip out on me while we're sleeping." He winked at Adam, as if he had read their minds.

"You're going to handcuff me?" Adam leaped to his feet and got into a defensive stance, slightly bladed, ready to either bolt right now or sock this jackass straight on the nose. He spotted Mony also rising, watching him for a sign of how to proceed.

"It's nothing personal, boy. Just trying to keep you safe. Keep all of us safe."

"But I didn't ditch you back at the lounge. You didn't need to fetter me then," Adam said desperately.

"You hadn't lost your girlfriend and your best friend yet. The stakes are different now. The script has changed."

Adam noticed the assassin had also unholstered his clipper and held the weapon behind his leg. But the man wouldn't kill him, right? He kept referring to Adam as the *prize*. Wound him, incapacitate him maybe. But certainly not kill him. Yet the man definitely would kill Mony if he thought he needed to make a clear statement. Maybe the clipper was for Mony and not Adam—an influencer to make Adam comply.

He couldn't risk seeing any more of his friends die; if the man killed Mony because Adam was not compliant. Plus, if Jonesy and Venus were truly dead, Adam would be the last of his cell of cyberpunks alive. And that certainly had never been the plan.

"Fine," Adam murmured and relaxed all his muscles.

"That's a good boy," the assassin said and pulled Adam's hands behind his back to secure the wrist fetters. "I only have one pair, but I'm pretty sure your friend here won't go off on her own without you. But if she does"—he eyed Mony—"her fate is no concern of mine. Your safety is all I care about."

"How am I supposed to sleep with my hands behind my back like this? And will this happen every night?" Adam asked, venom in his tone.

"I think we're all exhausted enough to sleep under any circumstances right now," the assassin replied and guided Adam to a mat that someone had laid out from the knapsack they carried.

Adam plopped onto the orange mat and eyed the assassin. "Does the place where we're going have a name? Something I may have heard of before?"

"The ancients had called it *Los Angeles*."

"And do *you* have a name?"

The assassin picked something from between his teeth with his pinky fingernail, then spat it onto the desert floor. "I am known as *the king*. The King of Los Angeles."

26

Orange incandescent bulbs burst to life overhead the two virtuality cages in the empty room where the slavebots had stored the teens, and Venus opened her eyes. Every muscle and tendon still burned from the electrocution in that guy's office. She looked over and saw Jonesy already wide awake, focused on who was coming through the door. The approaching footsteps and the dull hum from the orange lightbars that kept them imprisoned inside the cages were the only sounds in the room. Venus found herself holding her breath.

The large man from the office who had held the remote came into view. Venus panicked, her body responding immediately to seeing him again and expecting another round of shocks. Her heart thumped so loud that she heard it inside her ears.

Then she saw the two robots enter behind him, and she glanced at Jonesy. He too had brought his limbs closer to his body, expecting the worst.

The man stopped in front of the two cages. "I am going to let you out, but, if you so much as sneeze the wrong way, I have ordered these bots to shoot at their discretion. When I deactivate the shields, you will crawl from the cage and stand. Do you understand?"

Relieved that further electrocution was not in her immediate future, Venus nodded, almost enthusiastically.

She would comply with anything if it meant the man didn't shock her again. *Almost* anything.

The orange pulsing lights vanished on both cages, and the two teens crawled from underneath the covers and rose. Venus's hands trembled, and she couldn't seem to control her breathing. She focused on *in through the nose, out through the mouth.*

The tall man paced in front of them, his hands clasped behind his back. "The bots will escort you down to the processing floor."

Jonesy's eyes widened as he regarded Venus. They both knew what that meant.

"There, we will fit you with our lovely technology, then release you."

Venus had so many questions about Cyber-Corp's motive for taking this plan of action but was afraid to say anything—and the chances of him telling the truth were next to zero anyway.

The man narrowed his eyes at her. "You're probably wondering why we're not just killing you." The man moved onto staring at Jonesy. "Because I want you to experience, firsthand, the good we're doing here at Cyber-Corp. Once you understand the reason behind the *why*, I believe you will change your tune and will get on board. Maybe even convert your friends."

Did this man really think they were idiots? Venus thought. She didn't believe for one second that the motivation for releasing them was to convert them. This man had been warding off cyberpunks since the megacorporations had commandeered the country. Why would he go soft now? Cyberpunks were his sworn enemy.

Something more nefarious was happening here. And she didn't like the fact that she couldn't quite see the whole picture. She knew that Adam would have sensed what was really transpiring with this plan, but where was he? Was he even still alive? Had Mony made it out of the lounge too? Were they looking for her and Jonesy?

The two bots behind the man dragged Venus from her thoughts when they stepped forward and each grabbed a teen's wrist. She knew she had to relinquish to the bots; they were just too strong to retaliate against.

Venus fell in step behind the bot who escorted Jonesy, the man with the remote bringing up the rear. They exited the detention room, heading for a set of elevator doors at the end of the hallway. The two bots and three humans entered the elevator, and the man pushed a button labeled *B*. The lift descended into the annals of the building, deep below the ground floor.

The doors opened to reveal the largest room Venus had ever seen. She almost couldn't even see the walls on either side. Every ten feet or so was an orange chair, and above it was a contraption that had a mechanical arm and a needle at the end of it. The room was vacant of people, but the stations of chairs sprawled in all directions, each one identical.

Venus thought the stations resembled what she had seen in some books they had found during the railway car raids—something the ancients had used to sit in when they had their teeth examined, mixed with the contraption a doctor would use to check their eyesight.

"It's off-hours," the man explained. "If we were open, this place would be bustling with people, all excited to enhance their quality of life—and to get compensated handsomely for it too. It still boggles my mind that twerps like you are still out there who think what we are doing is *evil.*"

Jonesy shook his head at Venus to signal her to not respond. She realized it was what the man wanted; he was inciting them to argue their stance. She tried to imagine this hall during operating hours, bustling with people struggling to make ends meet to the point where they would sell their souls to a megacorporation just to put food on the table and a roof over their family's heads. And most of these people had a full-time job. She was sure the ancients never had this problem.

The bot that held her wrist spun her and pushed her into one of the surgical chairs. Jonesy followed seconds afterward, falling into the chair next to her, about ten feet to her right.

"The chairs don't have any restraints, as you two are the first involuntary customers to get the implant, so the slavebots will ensure you don't move or try to escape," the man explained, pacing in front of them, then stopped to glare at Venus. "I would highly advise not moving during the procedure. One slip during insertion, and your brain will turn to mush."

Venus noticed Jonesy's gaze darting all around, beholding anything within reach. What was he thinking? Fight back before they start the procedure? Could they each take their bot without getting killed? And, of course, the man with the remote wouldn't just sit idle and watch it happen. He would certainly jump into the melee, which pitted two unarmed teenagers against two metal-constructed bots with clipper guns and a grown man. The odds did not favor them.

Venus watched Jonesy relax and settle into his surgical chair. He must have made the same calculations as she had and had come to the same conclusions. It felt so, so wrong, but she realized their best bet for survival—and future revenge—was to comply and to get the implants and to be released. They could live to fight another day that way.

"If you don't move, this won't hurt at all," the man said. "You won't even feel it."

The two mechanical arms over their chairs sprung to life, whirring as they moved. They lowered, bringing the needle closer to the teens' necks. Venus closed her eyes tightly, just in case the man had lied about the pain. She held her breath and waited to feel the pinprick. Her muscles were taut, and she waited longer.

"All done," she heard the man say.

She opened her eyes. The mechanical arms had resumed their pre-surgery positions above the chairs. "That's it?"

"Told you that you wouldn't feel it. If we had made the procedure unpleasant, how could we get toddlers to sit still for it?"

Jonesy's eyes widened. "You install Synchestria Implants into children?"

"They are some of our best customers!" The man clapped, rolled himself onto his toes, then back to his heels in glee. "We pay the family double for children."

Venus's heart rate accelerated. She wanted to lunge from the chair and strangle this worm-of-a-man's neck.

The man turned and headed toward the elevators where they had come from. "The slavebots will see that you guys get out of the building. Where you go or what you do from there is on you. But mark my words"—the man spun to face them—"after you see how beneficial those implants are to your quality of life, you'll be back here, begging to thank me for opening your eyes. And your minds."

"We'll be back here only to destroy this whole operation and restore democracy!" Jonesy yelled, his boldness surprising Venus.

The man never slowed his pace nor turned around, just raised his right hand and gave the two cyberpunks the middle finger.

27

"Hello?" Clawdy called into the dim lounge. She maneuvered around overturned chairs and tipped tables. Something was not right. She inched closer to the bar counter and noticed all the broken bottles, the spilled orange liquor coloring the counter and the floor.

She spotted an open door at the end of a short hallway moving back and forth on its hinges. She assumed it was from the wind, but where would the air flow be coming from? She tiptoed behind the bar counter and down the short hallway, then slowly pushed open the door with her palm. As it crept outward, it exposed the carnage and more destruction that lay on the other side.

She clicked her tongue and swallowed hard as she gave a final push. She stood in the doorway, observing a large warehouse-size space, the far wall almost completely missing. That must have been where the wind was coming from, she surmised.

Her hand flung to cover mouth when she beheld the bodies. And the blood. And the limbs. All strung across the floor. She took one meek step inside the warehouse and scanned the area again. The floor looked like someone had tossed in gallons of red paint any which way, but she knew it was blood.

Clawdy stepped over a body, their intestines hanging loosely against their side and resting on the floor, like lava coming from the top of a volcano. Her heart hammered as her body shot full of adrenaline and gave her the courage to move onward. Bodies with no heads. Heads with no bodies. Innards flung around, no telling which person to whom they had belonged. A few eyeballs rested peacefully without their owners' skulls to keep them secured.

She surveyed the walls. Holes graffitied almost every inch, but the back wall that contained the rear door looked like a wrecking ball had gone through it. Thrice. She assumed that was where the survivors had run to, to escape the slaughter. She wondered who they were, why someone had attacked them, who that *someone* was, and where the survivors were now.

It was apparent and crystal-clear that whatever had happened here was a violation of Mother Dawn's will. As someone who was the people's voice of the deity, Clawdy felt it her duty to locate the survivors. Either help them restore their health or help them find the pathway to Mother Dawn's paradise.

She reached the back wall—or what remained of it— and exited the lounge. She surveyed the landscape ahead. She saw the large field, which turned into the desert beyond. She closed her eyes and tried to reconstruct what the survivors might have done after getting safely outside.

As if Mother Dawn had spoken directly to her—and, no, it wasn't the series of tones that overlaid until a single tone sounded—Clawdy opened her eyes and knew she would find them in the desert beyond the field.

She readjusted her duffel bag onto her shoulder and headed toward the wastelands.

28

Johnny Ray flopped onto his orange couch, poured himself a double, and activated his wall-to-wall tele-skin. The screens illuminated, filling with the images from the lead slavebot's eyes that functioned as camera. The neuro-trancer commune sprawled in front of him on the monitors, and he took a long pull from his glass. All he had to do was sit back and watch the destruction.

The neuro-trancers wouldn't know what hit them. And Johnny Ray had full confidence that what had happened at the Peppermint Lounge would not happen at the commune—nobody would escape *this* raid. Neuro-trancers weren't fighters, like the cyberpunks and rebels. The neuro-trancers were docile, obedient creatures. No match for an army of bots with clipper weapons. Heck, Johnny Ray didn't even think a single weapon existed on the commune, save for all the needles they used for the trancing process. And what would needles do to an army of metal giants?

The image on the tele-skin bounced right and left with each step the lead slavebot took and with each pivot of its head. The image of the commune's entryway filled Johnny ray's 360-degree monitors, and he saw the bot's arm extend to knock on the orange wooden door. Johnny Ray chuckled at the thought of how polite his murderous lead bot was, knocking instead of storming in, clippers a-blazing.

The door cracked open, and Johnny Ray didn't even have time to see the expression of the woman who answered. The lead slavebot pulled the trigger of his clipper in rapid succession, littering the first neuro-trancer with a pattern of holes.

The tele-skins filled with the army of bots, flanking the lead bot, now swarming around their commander and pouring through the entryway door and into the commune, firing at anything that moved. Or screamed.

0110000111110001110111001100

"Praise Mother ..." Cain didn't finish the mantra, letting the words fade and die as he heard what sounded like a barrage of shots.

And screaming.

He glanced at his trancing patient on the table and saw her eyes widen with terror.

"What is that?" she squeaked out.

"I'm not sure." He pulled his grime-covered goggles off his eyes and slapped them onto his forehead as he strode across the room, pushed aside the woman's heart monitor machine, and peered out the window.

He wiped sweat and a layer of orange dirt from his forehead with his sleeve and squinted. Fellow neuro-trancers screaming and falling where they stood filled the scene. He stepped backward and grabbed the side of the equipment tray for balance. He noticed, in his peripheral vision, that the woman had sat upright and was waiting for an answer.

"I–I need to lock the front door," he stuttered and bolted for the hallway, leaving her alone in the room, sitting on the table, one response away from entering Shangri-la.

Cain turned the corner from exiting the trancing room and into the hallway so fast that he skidded across the floor, and his right shoulder slammed into the far wall. He dug in his heels and beelined for the unlocked front door to the trancing complex. Screaming and clipper fire seemed to grow louder the closer he got to the front door.

But he heard less screaming. Were his brothers and sisters escaping the invasion, or were the intruders killing off his people?

And who were the intruders? Anti-religious nuts? That was the only answer that made sense to Cain. He couldn't think of anyone else on the planet who would dare desecrate Mother Dawn's ordained servants and their sacred land.

Cain reached the front door, placed his left palm on the orange wood, and reached for the locking mechanism with his right, until a hole splintered the door, sending him and wooden shrapnel backward from the blast. He landed on his backside, skidding a few feet down the hallway, and propped himself up with his palms.

His eyes widened when the door flung off its hinges, almost striking him in the head, and an orange metal robot, over ten feet tall and with just a dome for a head and two cameras for eyeballs, filled the doorframe.

Cain only had time to flip onto his hands and knees and start to rise to his feet when he heard the automatic fire of a clipper. And felt what could have been a thousand knives stabbing his back and neck as the rounds found their target.

He blinked out of consciousness before his lifeless body crashed to the hallway floor.

01100001111110001 11011100

Johnny Ray finished his double shot of liquor but didn't refill his glass. The action on his screens proved too riveting for him to peel away his gaze for a single second. He had assumed that the destruction of the neuro-trancer commune and the killing of all its inhabitants would be fairly effortless, but he hadn't expected it to be *this* easy. His mouth was agape, almost in disbelief about how systematically the slavebots had eradicated every single neuro-trancer. And within minutes.

The cyberpunks and rebels at the Peppermint Lounge may not have fought back, but they hadn't just laid down, rolled over, and accepted their fate either. Like how most of the neuro-trancers had. Sure, some had run screaming, but he really hoped it would have played out more like a sport— cat and mouse.

Nope. This had played out more like taking candy from a baby.

Slightly disappointed, after watching through multiple slavebots' eye cameras, he switched view to the leader again. The image of a closed wooden door filled the tele-skin. A white blast illuminated the screens when the bot's clipper fired, and a large hole remained. Through the hole, Johnny Ray saw a man on his back, grime-covered goggles falling off his forehead.

The bot kicked in the door, and the man spun to get to his feet. The sound and sight of clipper fire engulfed Johnny Ray's office as the monitors showed the man crumple to the hallway floor.

Then silence. And the bot turned motionless, following its programming to not move after they retired all their targets and to await for further orders from Cyber-Corp.

"Lancelot?" Johnny Ray asked.

"Yes, sir?"

"Are all the slavebots in standby mode?"

After a moment, Lancelot replied, "Yes, sir. All slavebots are awaiting my instructions after completing their mission."

Johnny Ray ran his tongue along his top row of teeth, his gaze still trained on his tele-skin, still filled with the motionless images of one neuro-trancer on the hallway floor, blood pooling from underneath him.

And complete silence from the commune.

He smiled when he realized all the neuro-trancers were dead. And now the boy with the blue eyes was safe from trancing, and Cyber-Corp could deal with him appropriately, without fear of him learning the truth about himself.

29

Someone shook Adam awake. He blinked to clear the cobwebs of slumber from his eyes and brain and saw the King of L.A. and the Peppermint Lounge barkeep standing over him.

"Get any sleep?" the assassin asked.

"A bit. No thanks to these fetters." Adam raised his hands as best he could, bound behind his back.

The King of L.A. leaned forward to uncuff Adam. "Hopefully we won't need them again. If we get to Los Angeles by midsun, you'll be safe and secure."

Adam groaned at the thought of more hefting across the wastelands for the next handful of hours.

The barkeep extended an orange canteen to Adam. "Drink. Slowly. We have to ration our water and food until we get there."

"Thank you, sir," Adam replied, accepting the gift.

"Elvis," the barkeep corrected, proffering a hand. "No *sir* around these parts."

He shook it. "I'm Adam. That's Mony." He looked down at his friend, still asleep on her mat. He thought she probably had a more restful sleep, as her hands hadn't been bound behind her back throughout the night.

"Mony, rise and shine," the King of L.A. yelled and nudged her with his orange boot.

She stirred and rolled over, then moaned in protest.

"We've got a long day ahead of us, but I promise the reward will be well worth the effort." The King of L.A. regarded Adam when he said, "And you'll love what you're gonna see. Trust me."

Mony got to her feet and shook like a wet dog to wake herself up. The other clusters of rebels were rising and collecting their personal effects to stow in the few knapsacks they had with them.

"Do they know we're coming?" Elvis asked the King of L.A.

"My communicator is out," the assassin answered, tapping his wrist to prove it. "But they should pick us up on the electro-scanners well before we get there."

Adam felt Elvis's gaze land on him. Then he heard the barkeep say, "That means they don't know about *him*."

"I'm hoping *no one* knows about him," the King of L.A. whispered, but still the two cyberpunks heard it.

Maybe it was watching this man kill Maggie in the subway. Maybe it was having a squad of killing robots shoot at him. Maybe it was not knowing if his girlfriend and his best friend were still alive. Maybe it was because he was sick of the riddles. Maybe it was because he had spent the night in the wastelands, handcuffed while he slept. Regardless, whatever it was, something snapped inside Adam, and he screamed, "What is so friggin' special about me? You either tell me now, or I'm not taking another step with you!"

Adam noticed the people in their band had stopped packing their stuff and stared at him. Did these people know too? Were they in on the secrecy? But it wasn't the assassin who stepped in to settle Adam's mind.

Elvis placed both hands on the boy's shoulders and lowered himself to eye level. In the fatherliest tone Adam hadn't heard from another male since his own father had visited the neuro-trancer commune and never returned, the barkeep said, "Son, you are very important. And we have vowed to keep you safe. Even if that means losing our own lives. But explaining it to you now, out here in the open, could put the lives of millions in danger. You are carrying a burden that you didn't even know you were carrying, nor one you asked for. But the multiverse has blessed you with the prize. And it's our job to get you to the finish line. If you could dig deep and find just a smidgen of trust in us, I promise we will protect you."

Adam ran his tongue along his top row of teeth in contemplation. "Promise the same thing to Mony."

"Excuse me?" This time the King of L.A. spoke. "You don't get to order us—"

Elvis put a hand on the assassin's chest. "The promise of protection is extended to Mony. As well as your other friends, should we discover that they are still alive."

Adam had not been buying it nor planning to accept the offer, until the barkeep added Venus and Jonesy to the equation. Adam softened immediately, especially since Elvis had included it without Adam demanding it. Maybe their intentions were good. Maybe if Adam complied for as long as they needed, he would eventually get his answers—and maybe even reunite with Venus and Jonesy.

It was worth taking the chance. What other option did he really have?

Adam glared at the King of L.A. while he proffered his hand and addressed his answer to the barkeep. "Thank you for treating me like a human being." He watched the assassin scowl, then smirk.

"Kid's got moxie; I gotta give him that," Elvis said, chuckling, then slapped the King of L.A.'s arm. "Doesn't he?"

"I knew it was only a matter of time before he started to grow on me," the assassin replied and tousled Adam's hair.

Adam ducked, unsure if the King of L.A. had done it derogatorily or as a sign of affection. Adam guessed it didn't matter either way. What was important was that whatever hierarchy existed among this band of rebels seemed to be dissolving the farther into the wastelands they went and the closer they got to whatever this Los Angeles place was.

30

Venus grabbed Jonesy's hand and pulled him to run faster through the pathways of the city.

"Do we know where to start looking for Adam and the rest of the group?" he asked, his voice punctuated with each footfall toward Peppermint Lounge.

"We're not going to look for them first."

Jonesy snatched his hand from Venus's grasp and halted, making her stop and face his raised eyebrows and crossed arms. "Then where on Mother Dawn's orange earth are we going?"

"We gotta find a 3-11 Man."

Jonesy absentmindedly touched the insertion point in his neck where the mechanical arm had installed the Synchestria Implant.

Venus stepped closer to him, almost aggressively. "Do you want to be the reason why the rest of those who escaped wind up dying? Because *we*, cyberpunks, led the enemy right to their hideout?"

Jonesy shook his head. He cared about Adam's safety just as much as he cared about his own. And it would do no one any good if they led Cyber-Corp right to their doorstep. Wherever that may be right now.

"Do you have any leads on where we might find any?" he asked. "I haven't been tracking where they hide out anymore."

Venus surveyed the area for alleyways. "I'm hoping they haven't changed their process in the last year or so, when Maggie's parents made her get a Synchestria Implant, and I helped her find someone to remove it."

"Woah, Maggie used to have an implant?"

Venus met his gaze. "You … didn't know that?"

Jonesy shook his head.

"Cyber-Corp paid her parents double, since she was deaf. They thought they would get different variables from her. That's what made her run away and find me. Join us cyberpunks."

Jonesy glanced at the ground, perturbed. "I can't believe I never knew that about her." He remained silent for a moment while Venus scanned the area. "I miss her."

"Me too," Venus replied, then pointed. "There." She headed toward the corner of an orange building with a small alleyway between it and the building next door.

Jonesy followed her and stopped alongside her. "What do you see?"

Venus touched the corner of the building's orange brick. "See these marks? Eleven slashes horizontal, three slashes vertical through them?"

Jonesy nodded and didn't need further explanation. "3-11 Men."

Venus touched the scratch marks. "These are their calling cards. Most people who don't know about them just assume the weather made them or that they are natural to the bricks' pattern. But to ones in the know, it's a map." She turned to face him. "Only problem is, how long ago? They could have left this location a long time ago. They are always on the move."

"Doesn't hurt to check," Jonesy said.

Venus nodded and entered the dark alleyway, doors lining either side. "Now we need to look for those same marks somewhere around a doorway."

"Then what?" Jonesy asked, stepping over a heap of trash that had fallen from an overfilled trash receptacle.

"Then we knock and use the passphrase. Hopefully, the passphrase hasn't changed since when I used it with Maggie."

"And if it has?"

The lights from the main pathway were far enough behind them now inside the alleyway that the dim glow from behind the closed walls wasn't enough to see any 3-11 Men indicators, so Venus stopped to wait for their eyes to adjust.

"If it has, then they might kill us."

Jonesy groaned in the dark.

01100001111**1000111011100**

The Chameleon twins—one with a bandage covering his missing ear, one with the directives from Cyber-Corp— watched from the shadows across the main thoroughfare pathway at the two cyberpunks inspecting the corner of a building next to an alleyway.

"I think we're in business," the uninjured twin said. "And you should have seen how delightful it was to watch them get zapped in the virtuality cages."

"I missed the show, and that pisses me off," the injured twin retorted. "Stupid clipper round. I'm gonna kill that *Princess* of LA when we find him."

The first twin didn't respond. He squinted to focus better on the two teens as they entered the dim alleyway. He didn't say anything to his brother when he stepped from the shadows, head down, and trotted across the pathway where the cyberpunks had disappeared.

His injured brother followed, pressing the bandage to the side of his face so it wouldn't come loose and fall off as he ran.

They stopped at the corner of the alleyway and leaned against the building, looking inconspicuous to passersby. The twin watched the boy navigate over a pile of rubble and trash and thought he heard them discussing how the girl already had experience with the 3-11 Men. He touched his holstered clipper under his orange leather jacket to double check that it was still there.

The twin tapped his lips with the knuckle of his index finger as he concentrated on watching the teens search the doorways for the 3-11 Men's symbol. He thought he might just suggest that Mr. Broad pay him and his brother a one-time fee to let them scour the province for those marks, then to return to kill all the 3-11 Men once and for all. They were the underground surgeons, specializing in removing Synchestria Implants. Why wouldn't Cyber-Corp pay him big bucks to eliminate another thorn in the company's side?

He tucked that idea into the back of his mind and refocused when he saw the two cyberpunks stop at the fifth door down and square off in front of it. He signaled to his injured brother that it might be go-time.

His brother nodded, unholstered his clipper, and pressed it against the backside of his thigh to temporarily hide it.

The uninjured twin slowly entered the alleyway, his back against the brick wall of the building to remain hidden in the shadows, his orange boots landing heel to toe, to keep as silent as possible—like a trained assassin for sure. His brother fell in step behind him, and they squatted behind the overfilled trash receptacle a dozen feet from where the teens had stopped.

But the kids weren't knocking yet. He couldn't tell if the 3-11 Men markings were on the doorway or not from this distance, but he assumed the teens had seen something to make them stop and to focus on that door. He regulated his breathing to not make any additional noise. His brother crouched beside him, also as stealthily as what the ancients had called a *ninja* during the Age of Destruction.

He wondered if those ninjas of yesteryear would have been any match for the assassins of today. He chuckled internally when he thought how that couldn't be possible.

011000001111**1000111011100**

Venus paused, staring at the three vertical lines slicing through the eleven horizontal ones, next to the windowless doorway. She glanced at Jonesy. "Only one way to find out."

Jonesy touched the marks chiseled into the orange brick. "They still feel deep." He looked at Venus with hopeful eyes. "Doesn't seem to be old markings. These types of bricks erode really fast with the dust storms."

Venus chortled. "Thanks for the geology lesson."

"Still valuable to know," he murmured, a slight sound of hurt in his tone.

Venus inhaled deeply through her nose, held it, then released all the air through her mouth. "Okay, ready? Let's see if that passphrase still works." She knocked and stepped backward.

Silence.

Jonesy moved his attention from the door to Venus. "How long do we wait until we knock again? Maybe they didn't hear it."

Silence.

"Or maybe they have moved on already," she countered.

Silence.

Jonesy swallowed hard and took it upon himself to rap his knuckles on the door. From his peripheral vision, he saw Venus shoot him a look but chose not to acknowledge it. He stared straight ahead.

Silence.

"Blasted," Venus breathed. "All right, let's go look for more markings. I really was hoping this wouldn't turn into a hide-and-seek game. But they stay on the move for their own safety—"

The door cracked open. Just a sliver. They could only see the center of someone's pupil in the small space that had opened. "State your business," a man with a gruff voice commanded.

Venus rubbed her sweaty palms along her orange jeans to steel herself. "We have some items that we would like to dispose of." She glanced at Jonesy, hoping he wouldn't try to add his own two credits to what needed to be said.

"What is the passphrase?"

Venus felt relieved and more stressed simultaneously. She didn't think it was possible to have such contrasting emotions at the same time. She was relieved that the person on the other side of the door truly was a 3-11 Man—or else they wouldn't have asked for a passphrase—but terrified that she might have an older passphrase.

Venus could either recite the last passphrase she knew the 3-11 Men had been using and be allowed inside, or could use that passphrase and be killed on the spot for being a potential enemy spy for Cyber-Corp. The 3-11 Men do not play when it comes to suspicion of undercover infiltrators.

"Venus, say it," Jonesy whisper-barked.

"Have a good night," the man grumbled and started to close the door.

"Tomorrow people in a concrete kingdom," Venus blurted out, her heart hammering now that she had said the words. No taking it back now. She closed her eyes tightly—didn't want to see the flash from the clipper if the passphrase was outdated.

She heard the door creak open a bit more, and a hand waved them inside.

Jonesy blew past her, bumping her shoulder as she stood paralyzed, thanking Mother Dawn that it had worked.

Venus finally followed her friend into the 3-11 Men sanctuary, and the door closed behind them.

01100001111100011101 1100

The twin strained his ears to listen to the exchange between the girl and whoever had opened the door. Then he smiled from ear to ear when he heard what had allowed the teens inside.

He waited for the door to close, then faced his brother. "We'll give it a few minutes before we approach. Don't want to make it overly suspicious."

The other twin inspected the bandage covering his wound. "What if we wait too long, and they extract their implants before we get in there?"

The twin scratched his orange beard and glared at his brother, almost disappointed—almost questioning if his brother was losing his skill. "Do you really think the 3-11 Men will start surgery on two people without grilling them first? They are too suspicious of everyone."

His brother checked the clipper's readout to see how many rounds he had left before he needed to recharge the weapon. "Won't that make them even more suspicious of us?"

The twin guffawed. "All we need to do is to say the passphrase, and, as soon as they wave us in, we start shooting. Everyone dies but the teens."

His brother nodded.

"And hopefully this will send those *cyber-babies* a strong-enough message to not visit any other hideouts and head straight to the rest of their clan, if they don't want more bloodshed on their hands."

"So, what's the plan?"

"We knock, like she did, and whatever they say to us, we repeat the passphrase she used. Easy peasy."

0110000011111000111011100

"Have a seat," the owner of the gruff voice instructed the two cyberpunks.

Venus and Jonesy complied, lowering themselves into two orange cushioned chairs, not unlike the surgical chairs from Cyber-Corp that had mechanical arms. Venus scanned the room. A hallway branched from the back, a kitchen set off to the side, a small tele-skin in the corner, orange paint peeling from all the walls. And four 3-11 Men crammed onto an orange couch, with a rectangular table in front of it.

She swallowed hard and rubbed the insertion spot on her neck.

"Before we ask you why you want your devil chip removed," began one of the men with broad shoulders, sitting on the couch, "we want to know why you had the devil chip installed in the first place."

When he folded his hands in his lap, the other three on the couch with him followed suit. Venus thought they almost looked like replica holograms of each other, but how would that be possible?

She glanced at Jonesy for permission and for courage to open her mouth. He nodded, giving her the confidence to speak up. "Cyber-Corp kidnapped us after a raid at the Peppermint Lounge and forced us to get the implants—"

"Devil's chip," corrected the gruff-voiced one. "Call them what they are, and it will keep the disdain on your tongue."

Venus chuckled, feeling some tension fall away from her. They weren't any less intimidating, but something about the man correcting her to call the Synchestria Implants another term—a term that seemed so blasphemous—set her at ease that they were still fighting on the same side, fighting the good fight.

"We're cyberpunks," Jonesy added, sounding calm and confident. "They used some army of robots that we didn't even know existed and killed a lot of our people. The rest got away, but they snatched us and brought us to their main office."

"And then they just … let you go?" the one on the couch asked and crossed his legs—the other three making the same movement in sync with him.

Venus furrowed her brows at them, unable to figure out what made her so uneasy about how they all moved in unison. But when she opened her mouth to answer, someone knocked on the door.

The four 3-11 Men on the couch looked at each other, and the gruff-voiced one's eye narrowed on Venus. "Are you traveling with anyone else?"

She shook her head, adrenaline shooting through her veins. She sat atop her hands to hide the trembling; she didn't want them to see her nervousness, but something was amiss. Her eyes widened when realization set in.

"Don't open it," she whispered.

"Excuse you?" the one on the couch said, then the other three replicas all said it too, in unison.

"Cyber-Corp released us so they could track us to the rest of our group."

The gruff-voiced one's posture went ramrod rigid. And his gaze turned stern. "You knew they were tracking you, and you still came here for our help?" he growled with such venom that Venus shrunk in her chair.

"You may have brought death and destruction to our door, little girl," the one on the couch said, then wagged a *tsk-tsk* finger at her. The other three did not speak but also wagged the same finger at her.

"Unfortunately we can't ignore someone who might need our help, so I, at least, have to check." The gruff-voiced one, the one Venus now assumed was the leader, shuffled to the door and barely opened it, as he had done when Venus had knocked. "State your business."

Venus heard what sounded like the voice of the assassin that had been in the Cyber-Corp's office when she had been in the virtuality cage say, "Tomorrow people in a concrete kingdom."

Then everything happened like a whirlwind. She immediately realized it was the assassin and that he had made a grave mistake. He had used the timing of the passphrase in the wrong order, sending the 3-11 Men into defensive action.

Jonesy hit the floor when the leader tried to close the door, but the assassin kicked it in. Venus almost fell from her chair, eyes wide, when she saw the four 3-11 Men on the couch slide into themselves, forming a single person.

Sounds and flashes from clipper rounds filled the room, and she dove onto the floor next to Jonesy. She tapped his shoulder and pointed to the hallway. It was either take their chances to escape through the back or go through the assassin at the front door. The Peppermint Lounge all over again.

They belly-crawled toward the hallway, and Venus glanced over her shoulder to see the 3-11 Man—the one who had sucked the other three he had been sitting with into his body—in a dive that reminded her of something the ancients had called *Superman*. He landed and rolled, extracting a clipper, and returned fire.

The 3-11 Man leader clutched his chest, blood pooling through the cracks in his fingers, as he leaned against the wall. His chest heaved with each breath.

Venus knew he was a goner.

The assassin from Cyber-Corp stepped inside and made eye contact with Venus. Panic instructed her to *move*, so she dug her heels into the floor and bear-crawled for the hallway. The boot falls of the assassin grew louder as he approached, and she heard Jonesy shriek in pain. She looked behind her and saw the assassin, with one boot on Jonesy's back, pinning him to the floor, like some kind of hunting trophy, and his clipper pointed at the back of Jonesy's head.

"Make another move, and I kill him."

Venus looked at Jonesy, whose eyes were pleading with her to stop and to obey. Then she flinched when more clipper rounds went off behind the assassin. Who the heck was still in here?

Rising above the assassin was his twin, holstering his clipper. And when he spoke, he sounded just like the first assassin. "The one who jumped off the couch won't be a bother anymore." He smiled when he raised the decapitated head of the 3-11 Man who had been sitting on the couch to show Venus.

She let her head collapse into her arms, her body sinking into the floor, accepting defeat. This time.

"Good, good," the assassin said. "My brother and I will be one step behind you the whole way, invisible. And this will be the outcome every single time you try to have someone remove your implants. Unless you don't want to leave a wake of corpses behind you on your way to your friends, I suggest you steer clear of any more detours."

He removed his boot from Jonesy's back, and the teen responded with a groan. The assassins turned to leave the apartment, and the twin with the bandaged ear tossed the 3-11 Man's head into the kitchen, where it struck something on the counter and toppled the item onto the floor, making a clattering noise.

"Well, it's a shame he didn't die in the subway," Jonesy said.

Venus rose to her feet, just as the twins disappeared through the opened front door, and spotted the two bodies on the floor—one riddled with clipper rounds, the other with a missing head. She furrowed her brows when the decapitated one shimmered and twitched. Then the three who had merged with him on the couch spilled from his body, now all four lying on the floor, headless.

She refused to peek into the kitchen on her way out of the apartment to see if now four bodiless heads were in there.

011000011111000111011100

Venus and Jonesy stood at the entrance to the Peppermint Lounge.

"I don't wanna go back in there," Jonesy said.

"Me neither. Let's go around to the back to see if we can find anything that might tip us off to where they went after they escaped."

Jonesy nodded, relieved that neither of them wanted to walk through the carnage that probably still lay inside. Including Cherie's body. They circled the building and found the shot-out rear wall and the door that everyone had fled through.

Venus covered her eyes to survey the landscape, then froze. A smile tugged at her lips when she pointed out yonder. "Look."

Jonesy came alongside her. "What?"

"Footprints." She turned to scan the ground behind her, and her gaze followed the clusters of footprints from the doorway and into the dirt and dust beyond the city limits. "They went into the wastelands."

"We should follow."

"If the wind hasn't covered their footprints yet, we should be able to follow them until we reach them."

The cyberpunks took their first steps toward the wastelands.

"We don't know how far ahead of us they are. We will never catch up with them, unless they stopped moving."

Venus scratched the back of her head and inclined her chin. "What's on the other side of the wastelands?"

"No idea." Jonesy kept his gaze trained on the footprints in the ground. "Nobody I know has ever gone that far."

The teens shuffled along the barren terrain, the city growing smaller behind them, the expanse of the wastelands growing larger in front of them.

"Let's just stick to following their trail, and, if we try to push through and not sleep, we might catch up to them, especially if they stopped to rest."

"That plan sounds amazing and terrible all at the same time," Jonesy said, chuckling and rubbing the spot where Cyber-Corp had inserted the implant. "And won't the assassin duo be following us? And isn't Cyber-Corp tracking us? This all feels incredibly unsafe, out in the wastelands, like sitting ducks."

Venus grabbed his hand to comfort him and to show confidence. "If the assassins wanted to kill us, they would have in the apartment of the 3-11 Men. The twin assassin made it clear. They won't harm us, as long as we are moving toward the rest of our group."

"I get that. But aren't we leading them straight to Adam and everyone, making it easy for them to send more killer robots? Like, *Here you go. Here's the rest of the ones you didn't kill the first time.*"

Venus halted and spun to face him, their hands letting go of each other. "Look. It sounds absolutely suicidal on the surface. Don't you think I know that? But how long have you been friends with Adam?"

Jonesy scratched his forehead. "Pretty much all my life. He's been my only friend. Until I met the rest of you guys, of course."

"Then you must have felt drawn to him also. Felt something was special about him. Something … safe and also absolute. And I'm not just talking about the fact that in a world of only orange-eyed people, he has blue eyes. While that adds to it, don't you just feel … untouchable around him?"

Jonesy side-eyed her and lowered his head a smidgen. "So, is *that* why you fell in love with him? Why you wanted to be his girlfriend? Because you think he's more special than anyone else?"

Venus chortled. "Isn't that why anyone wants to be with someone, because they see something special in them?"

"You know what I mean," Jonesy said in almost a bark. "That's my best friend. And I truly hope I'm not standing here and hearing that the girl he loves is only with him because she thinks he has some divine powers or something."

Venus shook her head. "I never went as so far to say *powers*. And I love Adam because I fell in love with his personality and his tenderness and his confidence and his kindness. I fell in love with him as a person. It wasn't until afterward that I felt this … aura around him that I can't explain. It's this energy. It's different."

Venus went to turn forward again so they could continue their trek into the wastelands, but movement back toward the Peppermint Lounge caught her eye. She glanced over her shoulder to confirm her suspicions.

Yep. The twin assassins had fallen in step behind the two cyberpunks. She realized she and Jonesy would just have to be okay knowing that two trained killers would be on their tail throughout their journey across a completely barren landscape, with no place to hide or to take cover.

At least she knew their plan was to keep her and Jonesy alive. Until she reunited with the rest of the group. Then she knew all bets were off—and everything would be left to chance.

Unless, of course, her intuitions about Adam were true, and he did have the ability to save them all.

31

The King of L.A. raised a fist above his head to signal for the convoy to stop. Elvis came alongside him, Adam and Mony stopping behind the assassin. The rest of their troop halted too.

Adam scanned the area and wondered why they had stopped at such a nondescript spot. The wastelands surrounded them as far as the eye could see. Straight ahead seemed like an infinite number of miles of nothingness and barren topography.

Adam watched the travelers stand their ground, the energy among them almost palpable. What was going on? He glanced at Mony, and she shrugged, both palms facing skyward, as if to say, *Beats me.*

Silence consumed them. When Adam turned his head, the wind made a different frequency in his eardrum but, other than that, stillness. With every passing second, he was scared to make a noise or a movement, to throw off whatever bizarre ritual might be happening right now.

The King of L.A., standing in front of Adam, slowly lowered his closed fist and rested it by his side. Then he side-eyed Elvis, the barkeep. "They do see us, right?"

Adam thought the man meant everyone in the troop behind him. Of course they see him. What a weird thing to—

The landscape in front of the assassin moved upward and away, as if the ground had been painted on a dome, and the dome was opening. And the farther it rose in the air, the opening between the rising land and what now was the real ground exposed a cityscape that made Adam slap his hand over his gaping mouth.

As the desert rose into the air, like someone pulling window blinds—clearly now just an illusion—and exposed the wonders beyond, Adam stepped backward, overwhelmed at the sights. And the colors!

Where the wastelands used to reside, a city lay before them. Vibrant yellows, blues, oranges, purples, and greens adorned all the people's wardrobes. Pedestrians crammed the sidewalks, and multicolored moving vehicles with wheels taller than Adam traversed the pathways—or were they called *streets* here? The buildings, donning resplendent neon signs that flashed every color of the rainbow and then some, stretched far into the bluest sky Adam had ever seen. He could not spot a speck of dirt or dust anywhere. The curtain had been raised, revealing an entirely different universe.

The King of L.A. turned to face Adam and Mony, a smile stretching ear to ear, creasing the crow's feet around his eyes even deeper. "Welcome, my dear cyberpunks, to the greatest kept secret in the country. I give you, Los Angeles."

Adam slowly turned to Mony, his eyebrows as high as they could rise. "What the …?"

"Come, come. They can't leave the mirage dome open forever." The King of L.A. moved forward, stepping from orange desert dust and crossing into the cleanest and most vibrant place that ever could live in Adam's wildest dreams.

Once the small band of rebels had moved beyond the desert and into the city, the dome closed the same way it had opened. Because they were inside the city now, what they saw behind them—where they had come from—was not desert but an illusion of the extension of the city, sprawling forever in that direction. When the dome clicked and securely closed, a city of the brightest lights enveloped the cyberpunks, hiding them completely from the world they had just stepped out of.

But also from any girlfriend's or best friend's eyes who might be searching for them also.

01100001 1111 1000111011100

Elvis whispered something into the King of L.A.'s ear, and the assassin nodded. He turned to face the group behind him. "All of you have been here before, save two." He eyed Adam and Mony and winked at them playfully. "So you know the rules. Go in safety. I have some introductions to make with our newcomers. I advise all of you to not leave the city until we've figured this all out and until we know what we're dealing with."

The small horde of rebels nodded in understanding and slowly dispersed, leaving the assassin, Elvis, and the two cyberpunks standing there alone.

"I know. I know. You guys have a million and one questions," the King of L.A. said, rubbing his hands together, almost in childlike excitement. "You will learn all the answers to your questions without having to ask anything if you have patience. Now, come. Lots to teach you."

The assassin turned and joined the flow of pedestrians, Elvis walking side by side with him, the two teens trying to keep up through the congestion of city folk. Adam looked up and around, beholding the sights and the sounds of a place that he had only read about in the journals of the ancients. How did a city like this still exist in the provinces?

And he didn't think he would ever see such glorious colors with his own eyes.

Vehicles created traffic jams in front of him, and while he was sure the operators—no, *drivers* were what the ancients had called them—were probably upset at the inconvenience, he marveled at the driving machines with giddiness. He particularly liked the ones with strips of bright yellow or neon pink lights glowing underneath or encircling their wheels.

He turned his focus to the pedestrians on the sidewalk, all dressed in shiny suits or flamboyant colors—a smorgasbord of rainbows on their clothes. Many wore flat sunglasses adorned with colorful stripes across the lenses. It was so magnificent that he wanted to clap and applaud the splash of colors across everything he saw.

Just to ensure this was reality, he glanced behind him, expecting to see the barrenness of the wastelands, but, nope, the resplendent cityscape extended in all directions. And the stores and the buildings too. He thought there were as many LED lights on this single strip as there were in the rest of the country cumulatively. Neon signs, changing colors as the lights flickered, advertised their wares. Some had yellow moving lights on arrows, pointing to a door that boasted the hottest women and men you could feast your eyes upon, for a price.

Adam quickly sidestepped someone his age, dressed in a lavender-colored jumpsuit, with flashing lights going up and down the side of their legs, wearing sunglasses with slits instead of lenses. The teen breezed by on a bright green rectangular board that hovered about six inches off the ground. He wove in and out of the people on the sidewalk, then scooted across the street, maneuvering around the vehicles—some honking a loud horn at him.

Adam never wanted to leave this place.

"Are we dreaming?" Mony asked next to him.

He had forgotten she was there, so consumed with the foreign sights and colors surrounding him in this bustling city. "I–I don't think so."

The King of L.A. turned slightly but never slowed his pace to talk to the two cyberpunks. "Up there. That's where we're going." He pointed farther ahead, about two buildings away.

They stopped at the edge of a curb, a light across the street telling them to wait. Adam had never experienced traffic control. He didn't want anyone to realize this was abnormal for him—didn't want to look like a tourist—so he crammed his hands into his pockets, like waiting to cross was the most natural thing in the world. He saw the figure on the sign change from red to white, and everyone around him headed to cross the street, the moving vehicles stopping. He glanced up and saw a vertical string of lights. The top one illuminated red. He followed the crowd, staying behind the King of L.A. and Elvis, next to Mony.

They reached the front of the building that marked their destination, and the assassin stopped and faced Adam. "When they get a good look at you, they will treat you differently. We'll explain everything, but I wanted you to be prepared for their reaction."

"All because of my eye color?"

"Oh no, boy. It's so, so much more than that."

01100001111000111011100

Adam and Mony followed the King of L.A. and Elvis into the lobby, and the assassin gave a thumbs-up to a young woman behind a desk. She smiled at him and pushed a button. Elevator doors opened to their right. They entered the lift, and the doors closed.

"We call this building the *Concrete Kingdom*. It's the capital, if you will, of Los Angeles. And the citizens here refer to themselves as *tomorrow people*. Cloaking technology, called the mirage dome, completely masks us from the outside world. That's why you couldn't see it, but we can see out." The elevator shook to life and rose. "All the most brilliant minds work in here, tirelessly trying to connect the dots."

"The dots?" Mony asked.

The King of L.A. grinned. "I told you. All in good time."

The elevator stopped rising, and the doors opened to expose an enormous domed room. Tele-skins covered every inch from waist up. Keyboards, flashing buttons, and joysticks covered every inch from waist down, with a person sitting in front of the consoles every five feet or so. Machines that Adam recognized as "computer towers" from the Age of Destruction lay stacked upon themselves in one corner, all blinking green, confirming they were operating.

The King of L.A. bustled from the elevator and into the middle of the circular room like he owned the place. Adam and Mony hesitated.

"It's fine. They won't bite," Elvis said.

The cyberpunks followed the barkeep into the center of the room. Adam looked down to see that the flooring was metal grates. He could see through and down, down, down as many floors as they had ascended to get here. Vertigo swam in his head, and he redirected his gaze to the circular tele-skin that surrounded him.

The King of L.A. stood next to a man in a sun-yellow lab coat, almost making Adam's eyes hurt from its brightest. "I'd like you to meet someone," the assassin said. "This is Doctor R."

The short man, with glasses so thick that his eyes looked like pinpricks and with thinning hair combed over to hide a balding spot, proffered a hand.

"It's nice to meet you," Adam said and gripped the doctor's hand.

Doctor R stopped mid shake and pulled Adam in close. "My boy, you really are the prize." He grabbed Adam's face so he could manipulate the angle to inspect the teen's eyes.

Adam wrestled between allowing this man of obvious high stature in a land that seemed mystical to manhandle his face or slapping away the hand in disgust. He chose to let it play out, since all of this seemed like a dream.

Doctor R quickly pivoted his head to face the King of L.A. "He doesn't know, does he?"

The assassin shook his head.

"Oh, boy, you are in for a ride," the doctor said to Adam. "You are what we've been waiting for."

Adam didn't like the ominousness of those words or the man's tone, but he found that he trusted the King of L.A. at this point, for better or for worse.

Then, as if Mother Dawn herself had hit Pause, everyone in the control room halted in their tracks—some mid stride, some with a pen frozen in mid notetaking—as they homed in on his face, the lack of movement now shrouding the area in complete silence.

No, not his face, he knew. His ice-blue eyes.

A female technician's calculator that had been balancing on a clipboard slid to the metal floor with a clatter. The sound brought everyone out of their reverie, and she apologized as she bent to collect the fallen instrument.

"Remain professional, people," Elvis scolded. "I'll hold a briefing to explain everything in detail to you all when I cut our guests loose soon to have some chow."

The technicians in lab coats slowly resumed their duties, albeit sometimes glancing over their shoulder to gawk at the freak, like he was some sideshow attraction in one of those Carnival of Oddities he had read that the ancients used to tour from town to town.

Doctor R put his arm around Adam's shoulders and stood next to him. "Who's your friend?" he whispered.

Adam snuck a peek at Mony, standing next to him. "You mean, *her*?"

"*Uh-huh.* Can she be trusted?"

Without hesitation, Adam replied, "If you can't say what you need to say to her, then I don't want to hear it."

Doctor R smiled. "That's what I wanted to hear."

"And you can promise her safety?" Adam asked.

Doctor R threw back his head and let out an obnoxious, mocking laugh. "My son, she remains safe as long as *you* say she should. Now, before I blow wide open everything you thought you knew about life, do you have any questions?"

Adam wanted the man to remove his arm from his shoulders, as it felt aggressive and intimidating, but he thought it would be rude to shrug it off, so he focused on the questions he had. "Where are we?"

"Los Angeles, boy. I'd assumed my freedom-fighting friend would have at least told you that."

"No," Adam said. "Where *are* we? We were in the desert, then this whole hidden world appeared."

Adam was thankful when the man removed his arm from Adam's shoulders and paced in front of him instead. "Out there is the illusion. In here is the reality."

"I don't even know what that means," Adam said, looking at Mony for backup.

She shook her head.

Doctor R sucked in his top lip and raised an eyebrow at the King of L.A. "It's your call. Do we tell him everything now and see how he takes it, or do you want to do increments, baby steps?"

From behind Adam and Mony, the assassin replied, "I see no benefit in telling him in pieces. The time has come for him to know the truth." He made eye contact with Adam. "That's if he's ready to hear it because, once he knows, he'll have to make the hardest decision of his life."

Mony placed a hand on Adam's shoulder for reassurance.

Adam took a deep breath, surveyed the domed metal room of monitors and all these people in lab coats, remembered the brightness of the city outside and its residents, all clearly not belonging to the world he thought existed.

Then Adam nodded.

32

Venus thought her thighs were on fire and couldn't imagine taking another step through the wastelands, the heat of the sun beating atop their heads. She couldn't remember the last time they had eaten or had drunk anything. Surely it must have been in the Peppermint Lounge before the attack. Was that over twenty-four hours now? Gosh, even time seemed to be inconsistent out here.

Jonesy groaned with each step. Loudly. Normally that would annoy her to the point of scolding him and telling him to knock it off, but she felt every muscle in her body would be making the same noise if they could talk. So she chose to ignore him.

She kept her gaze on the orange dusty ground as they traveled so she could remain focused on the footprints. Why look straight ahead? The sun would just blind her, and the sprawling barren wastelands would just depress her more.

At least the same number of footsteps stayed consistent. Didn't look like they had lost anyone in the convoy during their journey.

Jonesy arm-barred her across her chest to get her to stop. She looked at him and saw he had his index finger vertical across his lips. *Shh.* Then he pointed straight ahead.

Venus panned her gaze to follow his finger and saw the backside of a small, mousy woman, with a duffel bag slung over her shoulder. She was going to each discarded canteen on the ground and checking for water, and, when finding nothing, she tossed the canteen onto the ground.

Venus pulled her lips into her mouth to help her think. Was this woman a threat? There was nowhere to hide out here, so they had to engage with her. Venus pumped her palm toward the ground to signal for Jonesy to remain here as Venus approached the woman from behind. She contemplated purposefully making noise so the woman knew they were here. It would remove the possibility of startling this woman, who could be armed and might just start firing.

So Venus cleared her throat obnoxiously loud.

The woman spun to face the sound, and Venus's eyes widened as she stepped backward. The round goggles on the woman's head? Venus knew only neuro-trancers wore those. But how did she get … out here in the wastelands?

Venus showed both palms to the woman to confirm that she wasn't armed or a threat.

"Oh, thank Mother Dawn, someone else is out here," the woman said.

Venus sighed in relief and relaxed.

Jonesy came alongside her , his hands on his hips.

"What are you doing out here?" Venus asked, trying her best to use a tone that wouldn't pose the question as accusatory or an interrogation.

"Here, specifically? Or here, outside the commune?"

"So, you are one …" Jonesy whispered, taking another step closer to the woman.

Venus felt this woman posed no threat—so far, at least—and closed the distance between them so they wouldn't have to yell to hear each other. When Venus was an arm's length from her, the woman reached out and grabbed Venus's hands. The cyberpunk didn't flinch; nothing about the woman's movements seemed threatening or aggressive.

"Child, do you have any water or food?"

Venus shook her head. "I was hoping we would find something out here. We don't know how much farther we have to travel, which scares the bejeesus out of me, because, if we don't find something soon, I don't think we can make it back to the city before dying."

The neuro-trancer nodded solemnly. "I feel I'm in the same boat. Name's Clawdy." She proffered a hand.

Venus and Jonesy shook it. "I'm Venus. This is Jonesy."

"With all due respect, ma'am, what are you doing out here?" Jonesy asked.

"Please drop the formalities. I won't have any talk like that. I found a bar, or something, that looked like a war had happened inside. Then something drew me into the wastelands to search for survivors."

Venus and Jonesy eyed each other. "You went inside and saw them? The bodies are still there?" Venus asked.

"We were part of that … *war*," Jonesy added.

"Oh?" Clawdy tilted her head at Jonesy.

"Yeah, these huge robots came in and shot at all of us. A dozen or so made it out the back door. The rest were killed."

"The robots snatched us up and brought us to Cyber-Corp so they could install Synchestria Implants into us."

Clawdy's eyes narrowed. "They *forced* you to get the implants?"

Venus nodded.

"That is an abomination against Mother Dawn."

Venus noticed the neuro-trancer's hands ball into fists—the first sign of aggression she had gotten from the woman.

"Why would they do that?" Clawdy asked.

"They want us to regroup with our friends so they can track us and finish the job," Jonesy offered.

"And you're gonna just … do exactly that?" Clawdy asked, flabbergasted. "Doesn't sound like you care about your friends."

Venus blew out her cheeks as she exhaled through her mouth in a loud sigh. "We tried to get the implants removed, but we have two assassins following us to ensure we don't. They killed the 3-11 Men who we visited."

"Is that them, way back there?" Clawdy looked over the teen's shoulder to something in the distance.

Venus turned, placed her hand over her eyebrows, and squinted. She could barely discern two men a few hundred yards behind them, just standing like two ominous statues in the barren landscape. She faced the neuro-trancer. "That's them. Promised they wouldn't interfere with our travels if we don't try to remove the implants and continue to move forward to find our friends."

"That certainly is a pickle they have you in," Clawdy said.

"We also were traveling with an assassin. Supposedly the most elite in the world," Jonesy said, "so if we can lure the twins to our friends, we are putting our faith in *our* assassin taking care of the twins quickly. Then we can find someone to remove the implants, while our friends find another location to hide in."

Venus side-eyed Jonesy. While they hadn't quite agreed on an exact course of action yet, that one certainly sounded as if he had been formulating it this whole time. She nodded in approval.

"I think they camped here, but they didn't seem to leave behind anything of substance. And definitely not any food or water," Clawdy said. "I say we rest here for a bit, wait for sunset, before we continue deeper into the wastelands. If we're already past the event horizon of turning back without food or water and surviving, looks like Mother Dawn has made the decision for us."

Venus not so much *lowered* herself to the ground but plopped to it, her body collapsing from exhaustion and thirst. "Why are you out here and not in the commune? I have never ever heard of a neuro-trancer leaving, not in hundreds of years."

The woman glanced back across the wastelands to espy the twin assassins. "A series of events, a domino effect if you will, caused me to flee. I would like to think I can do Mother Dawn's work more effectively outside the walls of the commune than confined inside it."

Venus got the hint that the woman wasn't ready to completely share her reasoning, and Venus respected that, so she asked a question that at least centered around herself and Jonesy. "Why are you helping us?"

Clawdy removed her neuro-trancer goggles from her forehead and set her duffel bag on the orange ground. "Mother Dawn obviously has put me in your path. I was drawn to enter that bar, drawn to explore the wastelands for survivors. We don't ask Mother Dawn, *Why*. We ask her, *What more can I do?*"

Jonesy rubbed the spot on his neck where that mechanical arm had inserted the implant. "Do you truly believe that? Even outside the commune?"

Venus shot him a look of daggers that implied, *Shut up. Don't be disrespectful.*

"It's okay, child," Clawdy said, as if she had heard Venus's silent scolding. Then she made eye contact with Jonesy while she found a spot to sit. "I ... am not sure what I believe anymore. But I'm holding on to the possibility that I might be wrong in questioning my faith. It's not Mother Dawn's responsibility to prove to me that she's real. As a neuro-trancer, it's my job to look inward and to find her again."

Venus realized the woman had just inadvertently revealed why she had left the commune—a neuro-trancer questioning their faith was like a cyberpunk thinking that the megacorporations weren't *that bad* anymore. Oil and water.

Venus laid on her side, facing where they had come from so she could see the twin assassins in the distance. It appeared that they too were resting, maintaining the same distance they had been during the trip across the wastelands.

She never thought she would be relaxed and peaceful enough to fall asleep, knowing two assassins were not only on her trail but within seeing distance, but this was not a normal circumstance, and she knew she was safe. Temporarily.

And Venus also felt calmer knowing they would be traveling with one of Mother Dawn's clergy—regardless of the woman's doubts.

Sleep came to the trio before the sun had time to disappear from the horizon.

33

Doctor R placed his hand on the shoulder of a female, who sat in front of a console and wore a lab coat, and leaned down to whisper into her ear. He stood upright and stepped backward, alongside Adam and Mony. "I want you to watch each tele-skin and tell me what common denominator you see."

The two cyberpunks looked up at the various screens and watched what had once been a single image now split into sections. And each section looked like a different city. But were they all locations in the West Coast Province? Or different cities around the country? Or were they cities in different parts of the world? Adam had never seen what other cities or other countries looked like. Heck, he only knew they existed because books had described them. Now that he thought about it, he wasn't even sure other countries existed anymore. The ancients had left behind those books centuries ago, during the Age of Destruction.

But then Adam saw the common denominator that Doctor R had mentioned. Each image of a different city/country/whatever had its own color. Adam stepped closer to the circle of screens, his eyes widening. He saw a city where everything was red, another where everything was yellow, another where everything was green. *Everything*—the people's clothes, the ground, the buildings, the lights … just as how everything outside this *Los Angeles* metropolis was orange. He spun slowly to behold all the screens. More cities doused in single colors: blue, indigo, violet, and one had as many colors as Los Angeles right here also had.

Doctor R must have realized Adam saw the commonality because he said, "And what eye color do you think all those people have?"

Adam's shoulders tensed, but he did not stop scanning the screens, taking in more colors than he had ever thought were imaginable. "I assume their eye color matches the color of their city."

"Correct. For the reality that is red, everyone has red eyes. For the green reality, everyone has green eyes. And this orange reality has people with…" He paused.

"Orange eyes," Mony muttered behind Adam.

"Except you," the King of L.A. added. "We have never found a person yet with a different eye color than their surrounding reality. Until you."

"Why is there one that is all the colors?" Mony asked, her eyebrows furrowing. "Is that here, in Los Angeles?"

"No. That is where I am from"—the King of L.A. patted his chest—"the *original* reality. The *real* Los Angeles."

Adam snapped from his trance of studying all those different cities he hadn't known existed, and the color each one added to the rainbow splashed across the screens. "Why do you keep saying *realities?*"

Doctor R eyed both the King of L.A. and Elvis, who stood slightly in the shadows, just observing.

The King of L.A. stroked his white beard and moved to stand in front of Adam. He placed both hands on Adam's shoulders. "Would you like to sit to hear this?"

Adam shook his head.

The assassin sniffed once and wiped his mouth with his shirt sleeve. "Okay. Suit yourself." He stepped away from the teen and spoke while perusing the screens that still showed the eight different realities. "Have you ever heard of parallel universes? A multiverse?"

"I read about them in the books of the ancients," Adam said.

The King of L.A. chuckled. "You call them *ancients*, but they never existed in any reality but the original one—mine. You just got leftover duplicates, replicas, of everything that happened in the past. None of it actually happened in your universes because your realities are only a handful of decades old."

"Do you really expect us to believe—" Mony started, but Elvis raised his hand to silence her.

"Let him finish. You can then decide to believe what you want."

The King of L.A. doffed his head in thanks to the barkeep. "None of the singularly colored universes existed until, in my universe, we invented a supercollider called"— he paused to watch the faces of the two teens when he said its name—"Mother Dawn."

Just as he expected, the cyberpunks went wide-eyed and glanced at each other. "I read about those colliders in the books," Adam said. "They were used—"

"*Are* used," the King of L.A. corrected. "In my universe, we use them every day. And what do you know about them?"

"I know one was called the Hadron Collider, and they were using it to smash together protons and other subatomic particles to try to recreate the secrets of the Big Bang, what the ancients ... *um*, people thought was the start of the universe."

"Very good." The King of L.A. nodded with a smile, pleased at the teen's knowledge. "But *my* Big Bang. Not yours. Yours comes *because* of the collider. The Hadron eventually gave all it could give, information- and research-wise, so we built a new one. One much more powerful, controlled by a quantum computer for faster calculations and probability equations."

"You lost me with *quantum computers*," Mony admitted.

"Regular computers function by using ones and zeros in a row, like two-dimensional writing, called binary code. A quantum computer can calculate code on top of itself, so three-dimensional functions."

Adam leaned toward Mony to clarify. "It's the difference between drawing something on a piece of paper or making a sculpture."

"Our new supercollider and quantum computer tandem, called *Mother Dawn*, exceeded our expectations."

"You keep saying *we* and *our*," Adam said. "I assume you were part of the team who built Mother Dawn?" And that was when it hit him, after saying the words *built Mother Dawn*. That meant what people had thought was a deity, their *god*, was really a computer that existed in an alternate reality? If this was the truth, everything that everyone knew was wrong. And Adam wasn't sure he was ready to hear that truth.

"I was one of the lead scientists, yes, who helped build Mother Dawn," the King of L.A. said.

"I thought you were half-assassin, half-freedom fighter," Mony said. "So if you're not, that meant you killed Maggie in vain." She took an aggressive step toward him.

So many confusing thoughts swarmed around Adam's head that he hadn't noticed Mony bow up to the man until she brushed past Adam. He grabbed her arm and pulled her backward to stand alongside him. "Just ... let's hear out the rest of this, before either of us fly off the handle."

The King of L.A. regarded the two teens with sympathetic eyes. "Our supercollider created a tachyon particle—something physicists said was impossible.

Scientists had theorized tachyons to be particles that could travel faster than the speed of light. While the Hadron Collider had been focusing on protons and such, we were trying to accelerate photons—the particles that make up light—beyond their natural speed. We thought getting beyond the fabric of the laws of physics might be what shows us what happened at the exact moment of the Big Bang. Maybe the Big Bang happened because of some event outside the laws of physics. So we then thought outside the box."

"Sounds like you're about to tell us that you got more than you bargained for," Adam said, feeling nauseated and a little lightheaded from all this new information.

The King of L.A. nodded. "We recorded one particle, which broke the speed of light for a nanosecond—a single tachyon. And, within that nanosecond, seven universes burst into existence inside her mainframe. That event is *your* universe's Big Bang, Adam, along with the other six realities."

Adam brought a fist to his mouth and pressed his knuckle against his lips as he surveyed the screens again. "Why does one color dominate each of the universes?"

Elvis stepped from the shadows to add to the palaver. "Light consists of seven primary colors. When light is refracted, the different colors can be extracted, and we can see them one by one. As the tachyonic event happened, Mother Dawn acted like a prism when it created the new universes. So, as each color was refracted and separated from the source photon, it used that particular color to create that universe. Seven colors. Seven new universes. Colors completely separated. All thanks to Mother Dawn."

"If Mother Dawn is really a computer, and these seven new universes exist within her, does that mean we are just simulations?" Mony asked and shot a wide-eyed look at Adam.

"You act upon free will and have a consciousness. Your universe is as real to you as the original is real to us," the King of L.A. explained. "Mother Dawn is not controlling your thoughts or actions. You just exist within her mainframe. She created you, just as the Big Bang created us. So, are we any more real than you?"

"But what if she turns off? Then we blip out of existence?" Mony asked.

The King of L.A. smiled, realizing the teens must be accepting their truths if they kept asking follow-up questions. "And what if our sun explodes? We blip out of existence. See? It's no different how we were created or how we can become extinct. What matters is our consciousness. Our ability to be self-aware as *people*. And we all have it. You are no less a person than I am."

"And Cyber-Corp exists in all the universes?" Mony scanned the screens again at the eight locations.

A pang of hurt and sadness shot through Adam when Mony said the megacorporation's name, reminding him that his girlfriend and his best friend could still possibly be out there somewhere. Or possibly dead. Guilt enveloped him that entering Los Angeles had distracted him from remembering Venus's and Jonesy's plight. But what good could Adam do if he didn't know where to even start searching for them? He closed his eyes and tried to send out good vibes into the universe that his two favorite people in the world were still alive and safe.

"Switch the tele-skins to monitoring the wastelands," Doctor R said. "Sorry. I don't feel comfortable not monitoring outside the border for longer than I have to."

The eight universes on the screens blipped and changed to a panoramic view of the wastelands just beyond the mirage dome.

"Cyber-Corp existing in all the universes was the result of sabotage and greed," the King of L.A. added. "The thing about quantum computers is they evolve. They are artificial intelligence, computing and calculating at a rate faster than we can even process thoughts—a *spiritual machine*, so to speak. While exciting to the scientific community, the speed of Mother Dawn's learning and experimenting would frighten the layman. Mother Dawn surprised us scientists too but also excited us when she created a technology where people's likes, dislikes, tastes, and opinions—everything nontangible and objectionable that make us who we are—could be recorded and collected."

A pit grew in Adam's stomach. "Synchestria Implants."

The King of L.A. pointed at him. "Right. But they weren't called that yet. They weren't called anything yet. Heck, only the coding for *how* to make them existed. Mother Dawn didn't make the implants. She just figured out how to do it. And the information was there for the taking."

"How did it fall into Cyber-Corp's hands?" Adam asked. "And if Mother Dawn created it in your universe, how are they here in ours?"

"Yeah," Mony said, her voice higher and louder than normal. "And how are *you* here if you supposedly are from a different universe? You had me there for a while." She wagged an accusatory finger at him. "While this whole … city is impressive—especially that mirage trick, and I don't know how you do that—it's just a bit much for me to swallow that you are some multiverse spaceman or something."

"I had a hard time believing him too," Doctor R said, still reviewing the security cameras on the tele-skins. "So I asked him to bring me something from his universe, something that doesn't exist here, to prove it."

"And what was that?" Mony asked, her mocking tone revealing she still wasn't buying it.

Doctor R walked to a cabinet hanging on the wall, typed in a code on the keypad, and it beeped and swung open. He reached in and removed a tome of a book, in flawless condition. Adam didn't think he had ever seen a book without tears, rips, stains, disintegrated pages, but this looked brand-new. Doctor R handed it to Mony, and she ran her hand along the cover, then flipped through its pristine pages.

Adam didn't have time to read the title before Mony thumbed through it. He tried to catch glimpses of passages as she flipped the pages, but his gaze couldn't catch full sentences, just unfamiliar words and names.

"Since Mother Dawn created the seven colored universes, she is the only deity any of you know about," the King of L.A. began. "So this book would never and could never exist here."

"What's the title?" Adam asked Mony.

She closed the book to reveal the cover again.

"The Bible? Never heard of it," Adam said.

"And you would never know about it. Not unless someone brings one from *my* universe."

0110000111111000111011100

Mony handed the book to Adam as the King of L.A. explained further, "In my universe, we've had many gods and goddesses. They were used to explain things in nature that humans hadn't figured out yet. They had a god for why the sun rose and set. A god for thunder. A god for storms at sea. But, as science prevailed, explanations replaced these gods. This book, the Bible, is an account of a god that still exists in my universe—your version of Mother Dawn."

Adam had never wanted to read a book as badly as he wanted to read this one. It trumped every piece of literature or history book the ancients had left behind. This was the zenith.

But the King of L.A.'s fingers wrapped around the tome and slid it from Adam's hand. "That's enough. We gotta keep it safe."

"But if something happened to it, couldn't you just bring another one here?" Adam asked.

"Easier said than done. Do you remember an earthquake about ten years ago? Collapsed about one third of the buildings in the country?"

Mony nodded. "I was in school when it happened. The roof fell on us. Three of my classmates died from that."

The King of L.A. tapped the Bible's cover. "That was a result from me smuggling this in here. I will not chance hurting anyone again." He handed the book to Doctor R for him to secure it once more in the locked cabinet.

Adam cursed under his breath, horrified at what the one-eyed man's actions had done to the country when he had been a kid. And to think this man had triggered the earthquake, and it not being a natural occurrence made it feel even more egregious.

Mony narrowed her eyes at him. "But what about when you come and go?"

"I am carbon-based, and I must travel in the nude. Any clothing would create the same effect. However, live tissue, Mother Dawn doesn't track."

Mony blushed at the thought of the older man zooming back and forth between universes in the buff.

Elvis appeared behind the two cyberpunks with sandwiches and drinks for them. Adam and Mony accepted the meal with zeal and stuffed the food into their mouths as the King of L.A. continued.

"One of the lead scientists, and a personal friend, a William Broad, stole the coding for that new technology, quit the research team, and started a company called Cyber-Corp. His last act before he disappeared? He wrote a new code into Mother Dawn, adding Cyber-Corp and a version of himself and his assistant, Johnny Ray, into every universe so he would have a monopoly on every single reality. If we can delete that code, Cyber-Corp will fall across the whole expansive multiverse. Fighting Cyber-Corp face-to-face is not the way to win this war. Removing that code from Mother Dawn deletes it."

"Then just go into her programming and delete it," Adam said around a mouthful of bread and processed meat. "If you know it's there, just isolate it and get rid of it." He quickly caught a chunk of chewed food that fell from his lips as he talked and shoved it back into his mouth.

"The rest of the team and I tried to do just that, but that prick had placed a kill switch in Mother Dawn. So it would not allow anyone to remove that code nor allow anyone to wipe her memory. So we need to first find a way to remove the kill switch."

"Find a way around the kill switch, delete the code that this Broad dude created for Cyber-Corp to exist in all universes, and viola? Cyber-Corp just … ceases to exist?" Adam asked.

The King of L.A. nodded and chuckled. "When you put it like that, it sounds so simple. But we've spent countless manhours, with the smartest and most revered scientists in the world, to try to crack the kill switch code. And to no avail. Until the answer came from the sun."

Mony stopped chewing and raised an eyebrow. "And just when I thought my existence couldn't get weirder."

"Almost twenty years ago, a massive solar flare took every computer offline for a millisecond, and, within that millisecond, Mother Dawn had a computer version of a stroke, got its universes mixed up at the exact moment a single baby was conceived, and bisected the conception across two universes simultaneously."

"What does that mean?" Mony asked.

"One of those babies shouldn't exist in the universe they were born in. Shouldn't exist at all, to be honest. A glitch. Like the Bible that I smuggled in, an anomaly is present here that transcends Mother Dawn's coding for these universes."

Elvis offered the teens some chocolate desserts, which they accepted without hesitation.

"I've spent almost twenty years looking for that anomaly," the King of L.A. said, his eyes glazing over with the weight of the task he had been handed. "Didn't know which universe the anomaly was in. Didn't know what I was looking for. I just knew I would know it when I saw it."

"And what did you find?" Adam asked tentatively, knowing the answer already but wanting to hear it aloud.

"I found you."

34

Lancelot's mechanical male voice interrupted the silence in Johnny Ray's office. "Sir, the Chameleon twins are trying to transmit a message. Allow or decline?"

"Allow."

"Very good, sir."

One of the twin's voices replaced Lancelot's in the hidden speakers around the office. "Checking in with an update."

"Glad to hear from you. Hope it's good news," Johnny Ray said.

"I would say it's expected news."

"Oh, were they that predictable?"

"Followed them to a 3-11 Man speakeasy in the city," the assassin said.

"And I assume you handled it appropriately."

"Let's just say a few less exist in the world now."

"Fantastic."

"And one was a splitter—four for the price of one."

"Bonus points. Bravo!" Johnny Ray clapped loudly. "Those bastards are hard to find and harder to kill."

"No match for us, sir."

"So, what's happening now?"

"We've followed the kids into the wastelands. They have set up camp for the night. We're about five hundred yards behind—totally still visible though."

"Do they plan to cross the wastelands? They'll never make it to the other side without gear and food."

"I'm not sure what their plan is to cross the desert. However, you're right. Neither them nor us will make it, if that's their goal. I was hoping you could help us out?"

"I'll take care of you. And them. Can't have our bait dying on us, can we?" Johnny Ray said. "Is that all?"

The speakers fell into silence, but he knew the connection was not lost.

"What is it? I know there's something else."

"They've picked up another traveler," one of the twins said hesitantly.

Johnny Ray leaned forward on his orange couch and turned his tele-skin to tracking mode. "What do you mean, another traveler?" He typed in the coordinates for the wastelands and found the two dots that signified the two cyberpunks, but a third mark was not present.

"A woman. She was already getting ready to camp for the night. They talked for a while, and that's where our cyberpunks are staying. With that woman."

"She doesn't have an implant. I can't track her. Why would a single person be in the middle of the wastelands? Any discernible marks about her?"

"We're too far back to make out anything specific, just that it's a female. And older."

"I'll send supplies and take some surveillance while they are sleeping. See if I can get a good-enough image to run a facial recognition on her."

"I appreciate it," the twin said. "So far, all is going to plan. I feel confident that we will be victorious, and those brats will wish they never tried to go up against such a powerful giant."

Johnny Ray chuckled. "That certainly is the plan. I'll brief the boss-man on the new development. Watch for those supplies and stay alert." He killed the connection, closed his eyes, and sighed. "Lancelot."

"Yes, sir."

"Send recorded message to Mr. Broad."

"Go ahead with it."

Johnny Ray dictated what he needed his boss to know, describing the situation. He signed off when he finished and couldn't help but feel a sense of uneasiness about the mystery woman. Something seemed not right.

35

The King of L.A. showed Adam and Mony to their quarters, then escorted them to the cafeteria. The three of them sat next to the floor-to-ceiling windows, overlooking the congested cityscape. Adam spied the traffic jam below—still wide-eyed at seeing moving vehicles for the first time. The vibrant shades and neon hues that blanketed not only all the buildings but the residents' attire and cars made him feel like he had fallen into a rainbow comprised of one hundred colors. He would be happy if he never saw orange again. Or at least true static orange. He would still welcome a nice burnt-orange or a tangerine tone.

The images on the billboards that littered the horizon, some obscured by the skyscrapers, all moved like tele-skins, advertising everything from food products, moving vehicle brands, clothing choices, restaurants, and even something called the Red-Light District.

Adam had tried to ask follow-up questions or to get the King of L.A. to expand on what he had meant when he had said that the assassin had been waiting for Adam, but the man had said that they had dumped enough new information into Adam's head for the time being. That he should eat and rest, before they finished blowing further wide open what Adam had assumed was reality. Because, according to Elvis, the last part of the reveal was the real doozy—whatever that meant.

Adam shoveled food into his mouth, lost in the realization that everything he had thought he had known about life had turned out to be an illusion and yet this resplendent picturesque city sprawled before him. He only faintly heard someone snapping in the distance. The sound grew louder as he came out of his trance. Then he realized it was coming from the assassin, who sat across from him.

"Earth to Adam," the King of L.A. said, still snapping his fingers. "Blink twice if you can hear me."

Mony giggled next to Adam as she brought her bubbly soda to her lips.

Adam shook the cobwebs from behind his eyes and apologized. "I was in a million different places at once."

"I could tell." The King of L.A. leaned back and pressed his palms together, as if in prayer. "It's a lot to process."

Before Adam could open his mouth to respond, he noticed Doctor R maneuvering hastily around tables to approach them. "I think something's up," Adam said to the assassin.

The King of L.A. stood when he saw Doctor R. Adam got the feeling it was unusual for the doctor to move this quickly.

"Picking up"—Doctor R raised a hand to signal he needed a moment to catch his breath from running here— "movement in the wastelands. People out there."

"What … people?" the King of L.A. asked.

"Looks like two teenagers with a woman."

Adam's heart erupted in his chest, and he stood so quickly that his chair tipped over backward, making enough noise for that side of the cafeteria's patrons to stop their chitchat and eating to glance at the commotion. "Is it a girl and a boy teen?" Adam asked so fast that the words almost came out atop each other.

Doctor R nodded. "The two teens have implants. And … the Chameleon twins are a few hundred yards back."

Mony rose too, just with a bit more control, and grabbed Adam's arm. "You think it's Venus and Jonesy?"

"It can't be," Adam whispered. "These teens have Synchestria Implants."

The King of L.A. placed his hand on Doctor R to turn him to walk toward the control center. Adam and Mony followed. As they strode through the hallways, Adam's anticipation and adrenaline coursed through his body. He kept thinking how it *couldn't* be Venus and Jonesy, all the way up until they burst through the door to the control center, and he saw the two most important people in his life on the monitors that encircled the room.

$$01100001111000111011100$$

The tele-skins had homed in on the campsite where Adam and the band of refugees had slept in the wastelands. And his heart felt like it had stopped. There she was. Venus was holding his best friend's hand, both fast asleep on the desert floor. They had survived. Somehow they had escaped the Peppermint Lounge massacre.

But that left three questions. One was inconsequential, the other two a bit more dire. Who was the woman with them? Why did they have implants? And did they know the twin assassins were right behind them? Adam felt like he might vomit from both relief and terror.

The King of L.A. crossed his arms. "Can we get a better facial recognition on the woman?"

The screens zoomed in, but the closer to the sleeping trio the cameras got, the more pixelated the details. "These cameras only have a range of a few miles."

"And where are the twins?"

The cameras pulled back and swept farther down the desert to reveal one twin sleeping on his side, while the other sat cross-legged, staring intently forward into the distance where the two cyberpunks and the woman slept.

"The twins are not in attack mode. They are tracking," the King of L.A. said. "Something bigger is going on here." He stepped closer to the monitors and squinted. "Are you sure Venus and Jonesy have implants?"

Doctor R leaned across a console and pressed a button. The image on the tele-skins switched from real life to grids, and right where the teens had been on the screen were now two blinking orange dots. "Those are implants." He hit the button again to show how the markers were in the exact spot, switching back to real life, where the cyberpunks were now visible, instead of the dots.

The King of L.A. rubbed his chin and bit the inside of his cheek. "The twins won't engage until they must. I'm confident in that. But what will trigger them to engage?" He rubbed his white beard. "Go back to the woman again."

The tele-skins focused on the sleeping woman, and the King of L.A. tilted his head. Adam panned from the tele-skin to the one-eyed assassin, then back to the screens, wondering what the man was looking for.

The room went dead silent. Doctor R and Elvis stood behind the trio of Adam, Mony, and the assassin. The lab coats manning the consoles also watched the screens, waiting for the next instruction.

The King of L.A. stumbled backward a step and pointed at the woman on the screen. He spun to look at Elvis, his face bright with shock. "Get two shock-riders ready, both with side seats. Now! We leave in five minutes." The assassin stormed toward the exit of the room.

Elvis followed in quick step behind him. "I take it we're going out there to get them?"

Adam strained to listen to the men's conversation as they got farther away from the control room. The last thing he could discern was the King of L.A. say, "Neuro-trancer."

36

The assassin and the barkeep stood in front of a large bay door, waiting for it to open. As it rose, the King of L.A. ducked underneath to save a few seconds of precious time. He and Elvis strode to the hangar where they stowed the shock-riders. They found two, side by side, each with side seats tucked and hidden away, and mounted the motorbikes. They had to lay forward, their stomachs perfectly parallel to the ground, to operate the bikes. Sleek colorful panels of yellow and orange hid any sign of an engine. Vibrant wheel covers of lavender and pink hid both tires from view. Other than the handlebars, the shock-riders looked like a fast-moving rainbow.

The engines roared to life, flooding the bay with a deafening rumble, and the King of L.A. zoomed from the hangar first, with the barkeep following. They dipped onto the city streets, weaving and accelerating around the commuters' vehicles. The engines hit a steady high-pitched whir as they topped off the shock-riders at 200 mph. Buildings and pedestrians passed in a blur, the bikes streaking toward the outskirts of Los Angeles in a gamut of colors, like lightning.

The King of L.A. watched where the dome should be rising to let them out of the city and into the wastelands, but nothing moved yet. He chanced a backward glance at Elvis and signaled to the man to get control to open the friggin' dome. He chanced taking one hand off the handlebar at this breakneck speed to point ahead.

Elvis nodded, and the assassin didn't risk not looking forward anymore. He continued his course, not slowing his shock-rider, and prayed the dome would start to open in the next fifteen seconds or they would either crash into it or would need to dump the motorbikes. At this speed, that would probably be the end of his time in this reality.

He darted his gaze to double check that his shock-rider did, indeed, have a side seat. He did the math in his head; they could squeeze the two teens into his side seat, and the neuro-trancer could ride in Elvis's. The shock-riders and their drivers covered the distance from where the boundaries of Los Angeles ended and the wastelands started, like a bullet made of a blur of colors.

Back ramrod straight, body parallel to the ground, the padding of the motorbike pushing into his chest and thighs from the gravitational force of the speed, the King of L.A. fixated on the small crease that appeared between the bottom of the dome and the desert floor. He threw a thumbs-up to Elvis behind him, squinted to stop sand and dust from getting into his eyes, and pushed the shock-rider a bit harder toward the wastelands—knowing, if the Chameleon twins discovered that the cyberpunks were traveling with a neuro-trancer, the cat-and-mouse game would quickly turn into a game of hunt or be hunted.

37

Images from the drone, carrying two sealed bags of supplies, filled Johnny Ray's tele-skins. He stood in the middle of his office, Mr. Broad leaning against the desk next to him, both with a glass of liquor to watch the delivery and to discover the mystery woman's identity. The screens showed the expanse of the wastelands moving quickly under the flying drone, the topography never changing.

Mr. Broad checked his watch and sighed in boredom and anticipation. "Lancelot?"

"Yes, sir?"

"Time of arrival for the drone, please."

The speakers embedded in the office walls remained silent for a moment, until Lancelot's electronic male voice answered, "Thirty seconds, sir."

Johnny Ray shot his boss a devilish smirk as Mr. Broad pushed himself off Johnny Ray's desk and stood straight while scanning the screens.

"There. The twins," Mr. Broad said, pointing at two small figures in the distance. "Lancelot."

"Yes, sir."

"Drop off the Chameleon twins' supplies, then continue to our bait and their traveling companion."

"Yes, sir."

They watched the drone get lower to the desert floor, flying a few feet above the ground. The image of one of the twins, lying on his side—obviously asleep, and the other sitting in a Zen-like state, motionless, yet pointed straight ahead to look farther in the distance—grew larger on the tele-skins. Johnny Ray now could decipher the twins' clothes and the back of their heads as the drone approached.

The meditating twin must have heard the incoming machine because he broke his statue-like posture and turned to look behind him. Johnny Ray saw him smile when he noticed the bag of supplies hanging below the drone.

The drone slowed and levitated just above the twin's head, and the assassin snatched one bag from the clasp underneath the machine. He waved and winked at the drone, sending the image to Johnny Ray's tele-skins. Then he shook his brother's shoulders until the sleeping assassin awoke.

The sleepy twin rubbed his eyes and rose. Johnny Ray and Mr. Broad watched as the realization engulfed the other twin when he saw the bag and the drone. The second twin nodded to the drone.

Mr. Broad said, "Lancelot."

"Yes, sir?"

"Transmit *You're welcome* through the drone to the twins."

"Message relaying now."

They waited a few moments, then the twins both smiled and gave a thumb-sup to the drone in response.

"Lancelot, have the drone proceed to our friends up ahead. Silently drop the supplies so we don't wake them. Don't want to spook them or set them off course—they are doing exactly what we need them to—but have the drone get as many images as possible of their new friend within a timely manner. No lollygagging."

"Yes, sir."

The images on the tele-skin from the drone's camera accelerated across the wastelands again as it left the twins' position and headed for the cyberpunks and their mystery companion. Within seconds, the two sleeping teens and a woman became clear. Johnny Rau and Mr. Broad watched the drone descend to only a few inches off the ground so that when it released its clasp on the bag, it would hit the sand with minimal sound. The drone released the supplies, and the bag tumbled onto the ground.

Johnny Ray hadn't realized he was holding his breath until enough time had passed to confirm that the drop-off had not disturbed any of the three's slumber.

"Lancelot, have the drone swing around and get a clear view of the woman."

The drone whirred higher into the air, arched over to the side, then slowly lowered itself again. Johnny Ray anxiously rubbed his index finger and thumb as the curvature of the landscape became horizontal, the drone leveling off with the sleeping woman.

As soon as Johnny Ray saw the goggles resting on the sleeping woman's forehead, he grabbed Mr. Broad's arm. "There's no way!"

Mr. Broad, calm and stoic, said, "Lancelot."

"Yes, sir?"

"Get the drone high enough in the sky where it can still send clear transmissions of the ground but where they won't notice it. And get the twins on the line. Immediately."

"Right away, sir."

Their view from the drone's camera on the tele-skin, as the drone climbed so fast, gave Johnny Ray a touch of vertigo, just standing in his office, watching the screens. The drone came to an abrupt halt way above the ground and focused its camera on the campsite. Johnny Ray could still discern the people below, even if they now looked as small as insects.

"Whatch'ya got, boss?" one of the twins asked, their voice coming through the speakers in the office.

"That *woman* is a neuro-trancer!"

"How is that poss—"

"Shut up and listen. You guys are to go and, without waking the brats, kill that wench. Leave her corpse there for them to find when they awake, then back off and get to a tactical position to keep trailing them. Do not engage with the teens. We'll watch from the drone." Mr. Broad ran a fingernail through an eyebrow in frustration.

"Do you think more escaped the commune?" Johnny Ray asked.

Mr. Broad shot him a stern, pointed look, as if he could snap his assistant's neck if he didn't tread lightly. "How the hell am I supposed to know? I don't see how any could have escaped the slavebots. But I also don't see why one would ever be wandering around off the commune on their own anyway."

"I don't like it. And I certainly don't like that she's traveling with our bait. Something doesn't add up. We're missing something, boss."

Mr. Broad balled both hands into fists. "And we better figure out what that is before this whole fiasco leads to Cyber-Corp's undoing."

38

Maggie screamed when the clipper round hit her, and Venus reached for her friend, trying to somehow stop the inevitable. Venus watched Maggie fall backward onto the train tracks below. Venus faced the assassin who had turned their peaceful subway platform into a warzone and saw his clipper unleash a spray of rounds right at Maggie. Venus tried to cover her deaf friend's face, but Venus was always too late. The rounds struck Maggie's face simultaneously as Venus snapped open her eyes, panting, her heart exploding from the recurring dream.

Confusion and fuzziness dissipated as Venus remembered where she was. It wasn't much better of a scenario; she was separated from her boyfriend and friend, on the run with a neuro-trancer, tracked by two assassins. Sometimes her dream of the subway platform felt more survivable than her real-life situation.

Venus slowly raised her head from the ground and realized she had fallen asleep holding Jonesy's hand. She welcomed these small acts of comfort. She slipped her hand from his, ever-so-gently, to not wake him, then checked on their neuro-trancer friend. All was quiet. All seemed peaceful. Until her stomach growled so loudly that she thought the sound would wake anyone and everyone who might be out here in wastelands.

Venus rolled onto her stomach to gaze into the distance, toward the horizon, toward where they were headed. Hopefully to catch up with the small band of rebels who had survived the Peppermint Lounge massacre. Hopefully back into Adam's arms and around Mony's warm smile.

From the corner of her eye, a foreign object caught her attention. A bag. Venus became deathly still. She had to think this one through. Was it a trap? Had the assassin twins sneaked upon them while they had been sleeping and left it? What if it held explosives, ready to detonate the moment she opened it? Her brain calculated all the options—pros and cons—of opening it or leaving it alone.

She glanced behind her to check on the twins and jumped to her feet faster than she thought she could move. "Jonesy! Wake up!"

Venus's eyes widened while watching the twin assassins in an almost full-out sprint toward them. With only a few hundred yards between them, it would only take a couple minutes—three tops—for them to be upon their campsite.

"Jonesy!" She kicked him in the side, and he grunted. Venus yelled, "Clawdy!"

The neuro-trancer stirred first.

"The assassins are heading our way. Fast!"

That was enough to rouse Jonesy and to get Clawdy to her feet. The three of them stood side by side, watching the fast-approaching trained killers sprinting toward them.

"Do we fight or run?" Jonesy asked.

Venus spied the bag. She no longer thought the twins had left it. Maybe they were coming *for* the bag. She squatted and, without hesitation or care of the consequences, unzipped the top. Rations of food and water spilled onto the ground.

"Mother Dawn be praised," Clawdy whispered.

Venus checked the twins' progress, then surveyed the food and water. "I think they're coming for this bag."

"But who left it?" Jonesy asked, almost in a panic.

"I don't know. I don't know what the hell is going on."

"At this moment, they are far enough away," he said. "We have a large lead on them if we run."

Venus nodded. "Load up your pockets with as much food as you can; sling as many canteens around your back as you can. Fifteen seconds tops, then we run."

Clawdy and Jonesy squatted and shoved what they could into their pockets.

"Oh, for Mother Dawn's sake, what the ever-living hell now?" Venus almost yelled.

Jonesy stopped pilfering the bag of supplies and stood. "What?"

Venus pointed in the distance, in the opposite direction from where the twins approached, toward where she had planned to run. "So, are we being boxed in? What *are* those things?"

Clawdy rose too, all three momentarily forgetting about the food and water at their feet, as well as the two assassins closing the gap behind them. They focused on two machines, decked out in colors they had only heard might exist in the world, with two people operating each, lying on their bellies, as if the moving machines were a bed.

"What do we do now?" Jonesy asked.

Venus glanced behind her and surmised they probably had another solid minute before the twins reached them. Maybe they'll just take the bag and leave Venus and her friends alone. She refocused on the two machines approaching at a rate that she didn't think was humanly possible, desert sand and dirt kicking up behind them like a tidal wave. She darted her gaze back and forth—assassins, machines, assassins, machines—and deduced that at the speed the rainbow machines were approaching against the rate the assassins were moving, both parties would reach the campsite at about the same time.

Then she saw the twins unholster their clippers as they ran. Nope, they certainly were not coming just for the bag of food and water.

She looked at Jonesy and didn't even think of the words before she said them. "We run toward them." And pointed toward the incoming foreign vehicles.

Jonesy nodded, and the three of them bolted forward, away from the twins flanking them. Then clipper rounds flew over their heads from behind.

"They're shooting at us!" Jonesy yelled.

"Ya think?" Venus yelled back. But then she realized the rounds were concentrated more toward the neuro-trancer. "Clawdy! Run and duck! And weave! They're shooting at *you*!"

The trio ran while slaloming, making it harder for clipper rounds to find purchase. Venus realized she had underestimated the speed of the rainbow vehicles because when she recentered her attention, the two machines turned and drifted into a skidding stop about ten yards ahead of them.

The two drivers raised their heads and dismounted in a flash.

Venus was so happy that she thought she would cry when she saw who was operating one of those machines.

0110000111110001110 11100

The King of L.A. pulled his clipper from the back of his waistband as he yelled, "Get down!" to the three people in front of him.

He waited for the two cyberpunks and the neuro-trancer to hit the sand before unloading a dozen rounds down range at the twins.

Elvis rolled to the right, unholstering his weapon, and the two men sprinted forward on an angle toward the incoming threat, looking like they were running to create the letter V in the sand with their footprints.

The uninjured twin broke off from his trajectory and headed sideways to engage the King of L.A.

"Take cover behind the shock-riders!" the King of L.A. yelled at them, still lying on the ground. He squeezed off another burst of suppression fire to buy them time to get behind the motorbikes.

Elvis still ran in a diagonal direction, sending controlled bursts of clipper fire toward the injured twin.

"Take out their legs!" the King of L.A. yelled to the barkeep.

A sudden stinging sensation punched him in his arm as a clipper round just nicked his bicep. He dropped to the ground, got into the prone position, aligned his target's legs within the clipper's sights, and let three rounds find their mark.

The twin folded over and collapsed onto the ground. He grabbed his leg, screaming.

The King of L.A. looked across the wastelands at the barkeep and watched him go to one knee, set his sights, then … he had to roll out of position as clipper rounds almost hit him center mass from the initially injured twin. The King of L.A. raised his clipper, confirmed the twin remained focused on Elvis's position, and let five rounds fly.

Two missed completely. Three struck the twin in the face in an explosion of blood spray, bone fragments, and brain matter. He landed on his back, muscles twitching as his nervous system sent the last few signals through his body. Then he became motionless.

Elvis scampered toward the dead twin's body to collect the assassin's clipper from the sand and secured it in his waistband.

The King of L.A. heard the first twin groaning in pain up ahead, still on the ground. He glanced back at the shock-riders to ensure the teens and the neuro-trancer were still safe. He saw three sets of eyes watching over the top of the motorbikes and almost chuckled.

"Let's go have a persuasive conversation with our friend down there," he called out to Elvis.

They approached the downed but still alive Chameleon twin and came together so they now walked shoulder to shoulder.

The twin, lying on his back, separated his legs to aim his clipper at them without having to get up. Both the King of L.A. and the barkeep leveled their clippers at the twin assassin.

"We've already killed your brother. I will not hesitate to kill you if I see that trigger finger so much as twitch," the King of L.A. said. "It would behoove you to put down the weapon."

The twin groaned loud enough for them to hear as he dropped the weapon to resume holding his legs, which had three holes in them.

The King of L.A. and Elvis reached the assassin, and the barkeep eyed his friend. "What do you want to do with him?"

"If he wants to live, he'll have a whole slew of questions to answer."

The twin glanced behind him from where he had come from, a dozen miles from civilization.

"You know what?" the King of L.A. began, followed by a chuckle. "If you really think you'll make it back to the city in the state you're in"—he wagged the clipper at the blood pouring from the man's legs—"go ahead. I won't kill you just to see how far you get."

The twin sighed and relaxed his body onto the ground, relinquishing any hope of escape, and eyed his clipper that he had abandoned to maintain pressure on his leg wounds.

The King of L.A. thought that looked almost impossible—two hands, three holes spouting blood. The math didn't add up, and he snickered.

"Why are you following my friends?"

The twin lifted one hand from a hole just long enough to flip the assassin the bird.

The King of L.A. kicked the twin's clipper across the desert floor, then stuck the heel of his boot into the hole that the twin couldn't cover—math and all that. The man wailed in pain, back arched, and removed his hands from the other two wounds to ball them into fists.

The King of L.A. ground his boot farther into the bloody hole. "Why. Are. You. Following. My. Friends?" he asked through gritted teeth.

The twin grabbed fistfuls of sand and flailed.

The King of L.A. removed his boot and rested his foot on the sand.

The man on the ground coughed and choked from the pain. He rolled onto his side, bringing his arm against his forehead, loose sand falling off and landing on his cheeks.

The King of L.A. shook his head at Elvis. "Ya know, I almost respect the man right now. I had him pegged for a whiny little tattletale if ever captured."

Elvis nodded and made an *mmm-hmm* noise in agreement.

"Staying true to the assassin's creed, wouldn't ya say?"

"I would say staying *really* true," Elvis replied.

The King of L.A. eyed the assassin on the ground. The man had stopped squirming and looked to be going into shock. "I would say that he *wants* to go out with his dignity."

"Uh-*yup*," the barkeep added. "Think we should send him off, free of disgrace?"

The King of L.A. raised his clipper to the twin's face.

"Okay, okay!" the assassin squeaked out, raising an opened palm toward the clipper, as if that would stop a round from hitting his face. "I'll tell you!"

The King of L.A. chortled as he lowered his weapon. "And just like that, you're so easily persuaded to turn your back on the creed. You really are more of a coward than I thought. Disgusting."

The twin lowered his hand shield. "What … What do you want to know?"

"For a third time, why are you following my friends?"

The twin mumbled something inaudible.

The King of L.A. stepped closer. "Couldn't hear ya, partner."

The same murmuring nonsense came, but the twin moved his right hand underneath his body.

The King of L.A. leaned forward, his chin now just above the twin's boot on the ground.

"I said," the twin retorted, loud and clear, then brought his hidden hand across his body and opened it to throw a fistful of sand into the King of L.A.'s eyes, while he kicked his boot upward, connecting with the assassin's chin.

The King of L.A. shoved his palms into his good eye to alleviate the sting from the sand and stumbled backward. Through natural tears and squinting, he saw the twin's silhouette roll for his discarded clipper. Then he heard the discharge from Elvis's weapon as the barkeep unloaded a barrage of fire into the twin.

The King of L.A. buckled at the waist, trying to flush out the sand trapped underneath his eyelids, the twin lying motionless a few yards away. "Sam hell! Are you okay?" he asked his friend and barely could see Elvis nod with a sinister grin—both parties unaware that Cyber-Corp was watching every movement from high above them.

39

"I don't care if the Chameleon twins live or die," Mr. Broad said, studying the unfolding events on the tele-skin. "I only care if that jackass twin says anything stupid to save his own hide."

"Isn't it against the assassin's creed to give your captor what they want?" Johnny Ray asked.

Mr. Broad took a long swallow on the liquid in his glass and smacked his lips. "You would think, but I'm starting to feel like they are all bark and no bite."

They watched the King of L.A. and his friend, both their clippers trained on the twin, converse with him. The drone was too far away to hear what they were saying, but they saw the twin having a tough time deciding which clipper wound to put pressure on next, since he only had two hands, and his legs had three holes.

The two men in the office remained silent as they watched three people have a conversation on the screens, without hearing the words.

Johnny Ray sighed and took a sip from his drink, wondering how long this would take. "I hope they kill him," Johnny Ray mumbled.

Mr. Broad eyed him. "Oh? What's working itself out in that brain of yours?"

Johnny Ray moved from standing alongside his boss to facing him. "Think of it. We have a drone in the air. One twin is dead. This one has three holes in his legs. He ain't running let alone walking anywhere for a while. If ever. If they kill him, they load our targets onto those motorbikes, and the drone follows them to their hideout. And if the drone loses them—"

"We can track them with the implants," Mr. Broad finished.

"We only needed the twins to ensure our kids didn't remove the implants or hide somewhere in the city. They are in full view in the wastelands now. Our drone can do the rest. I say kill the twin so we can follow them to where they have congregated. It's gotta be out in the wastelands somewhere. That's where the King of L.A. came from. The drone can map the coordinates, and we'll deploy every slavebot we have to the location."

"Total annihilation," Mr. Broad murmured.

"And the last neuro-trancer meets the same fate."

Johnny Ray couldn't help but notice how wide a smile came across his boss's face. Then he flinched when he watched the King of L.A.'s friend unload his clipper into the last-remaining Chameleon twin.

011000011111000111011100

The office became silent. The two men watched the King of L.A. and his friend turn toward their shock-riders, the one-eyed assassin clearly having some sight issues, as he kept making a fist and rubbing his good eye with his knuckles. They left the two dead Chameleon twins where they had fallen, with no regard for doing anything with the bodies.

"Lancelot, lower the drone just a bit," Mr. Broad said.

"Yes, sir."

The image of the ground on the tele-skins grew larger as the drone dropped, then stabilized again. They watched the two men unfold each of the shock-rider's side seats—a small side pod that connected to the motorbike but rested a few feet off the ground—and the two cyberpunks crammed into one and the neuro-trancer into the other. The King of L.A. and his friend mounted their rides, lying on their bellies, and made a U-turn to head back from where they had come.

"Lancelot, have the drone follow them. I don't care how far or how long it takes. Do not lose them."

"Very good, sir."

The camera accelerated as the drone flanked the two shock-riders and finally matched their speed above them. The sand that the motorbikes kicked up behind their thrusters created a curtain of orange, completely blocking any chance of looking back and seeing the campsite or the two dead assassins.

The soundless drone followed the two streaks of rainbow as they sped across the wastelands long enough for Cyber-Corp's two top dogs to consume an entire bottle of spirits, until Johnny Ray's eyes widened when he saw the desert ground rise.

The drone, still locked onto following orders, slowed to a stop with the shock-riders below, to allow the mirage dome to open.

"What in Mother Dawn's name is that?" Johnny Ray asked, each word elongating with disbelief.

"Clever, clever pricks. A mirage dome," Mr. Broad wagged a finger of the hand holding his glass at the tele-skins. "Right under our noses too."

The two men watched the dome open just enough to let the shock-riders and their passengers slip underneath the opening, then the image of the desert floor lowered again, until it became flush with the real desert floor.

"Lancelot," Mr. Broad started.

"Yes, sir?"

"Keep the drone hovering right there. Do not let it move an iota."

"Very good, sir."

Johnny Ray searched the tele-skin, then eyed his boss. "Their implant signal is gone."

Mr. Broad nodded once. "Mirage domes block all electrical signals behind it. An entire continent of implant frequencies could be hiding there, and we would never detect it when the dome is closed."

"So, what … is the plan?"

Mr. Broad smiled at his assistant, and, without breaking eye contact with Johnny Ray, he gave Lancelot the order. "Dispatch every slavebot we have, equipped with mortars and clippers, to the drone's coordinates, then wait for further instructions."

"Yes, sir," the mechanical male voice answered.

Mr. Broad set his glass on Johnny Ray's desk. "The plan is a lot of *ka-boom*."

"Won't they see the slavebots coming from miles away and prepare for an attack?"

Mr. Broad furrowed his brows at Johnny Ray. "You don't know how mirage domes work?"

"I don't even know what a mirage dome is."

Mr. Broad refocused on the tele-skins, which revealed a calm, undisturbed desert—as if a hidden city wasn't just below the drone. "Archaic technology by today's standards but still effective when used correctly. The dome doesn't work like a one-way mirror. They can't see through the dome itself. They are monitoring the outskirts of it through closed-circuit feeds but only with a range of a few miles."

"Cameras," Johnny Ray murmured, then smiled. "All too easy, *huh*?"

"Like I said. *Archaic*. Works great as a cloaking device but not so great when threatened."

"Especially against a neutralizer."

"Exactly. Now you're catching on," Mr. Broad said, rubbing his hands together in childlike excitement. "You said it best. All too easy."

40

Both shock-riders sideswiped into the bay and skidded to a halt. The five dismounted—the two cyberpunks and the neuro-trancer climbing from the two side cars—as Doctor R, Adam, and Mony trotted into the hangar.

When Adam saw Venus and Jonesy, he broke into a full-on sprint. He watched Venus's face light up with a smile as he approached and raised his arms. When he reached her, he collided his body with her into a hug, wrapping his whole being around her. He inhaled deeply, not believing she was really safe and alive.

He put her at an arm's length but still gripped her shoulders. "I missed you so, so much. I was so worried."

He saw Venus's eyes tear up, and she used the sleeve of her shirt to wipe them away. Then Adam focused on his best friend, gripped Jonesy's shoulder, and brought him in for a hug. Adam felt the weight of the world lift just slightly off his shoulders, being able to touch the two people who meant the most to him.

When he pulled back from Jonesy, he saw Mony and Venus in an embrace. Mony sounded like she was on the verge of cracking and letting all her dammed-up sobs flow freely.

The King of L.A. and Elvis stepped aside to reveal the newcomer. Adam watched the woman, donning round goggles on her forehead and a duffel bag on her shoulder, look around in wonder at all the colors inside the hangar. *Wait until she sees Los Angeles*, he thought.

Adam found Venus's hand and intertwined his fingers with hers. He wouldn't let her go again, even if it killed him.

The King of L.A. placed a hand behind the woman's back and nudged her forward into the reunited group. "This is Clawdy."

Venus slipped her fingers from Adam's grasp to hug the woman. "I'm so glad we made it out of there."

Adam saw the woman nod and return the gesture. Then she made eye contact with him and stumbled backward so violently that Venus had to catch her.

Clawdy pointed at Adam, then pressed her hand over her chest where her heart resided. She inched forward, wide-eyed. "My child, you are exquisite."

Adam blushed in the presence of the neuro-trancer, and he turned away. He had almost had enough of all the attention his blue eyes now received.

The King of L.A. wrapped an arm around Clawdy, escorted her forward until they were alongside Adam, and wrapped his other arm around the cyberpunk. "C'mon, we have a lot to discuss. The missing piece to this puzzle just arrived on our doorstep."

Adam reached his right hand backward toward Venus and wiggled his fingers, indicating he wanted her hand in his again. He smiled when he felt her fingers intertwine with his. Everything would be okay now. He just knew it.

01100000111110001110111100

The King of L.A. watched with his one good eye squinted at Clawdy, Venus, and Jonesy as they devoured the trays of food that the waitress in the Concrete Kingdom's mess hall had brought them. Adam knew he loved the cyberpunk sitting across from him, but her rate of shoveling food into her mouth, chewed meat tumbling from the side of her mouth, made him contemplate sliding under the table to stop from gagging and to hide from the other diner's judging eyes in response to Venus's improper etiquette.

"Oh, Mother Dawn, this is so *good*!" Venus said, then poured soda into her mouth that was still full of a heap of a smorgasbord of food items.

Jonesy ate just as fast, but at least he swallowed his food before putting more in his mouth.

Clawdy, dainty as ever, ate as if someone had clicked the slow-motion button on a remote pointed at her. She glanced at Venus and swallowed. "Do you still have absolute faith in Mother Dawn?"

That made the table go quiet, all eating stopped. Adam side-eyed the neuro-trancer.

"I mean, for me," Clawdy began, "I was told Mother Dawn existed, so I believed it. I was born into a neuro-trancer family. Indoctrinated. But I also never knew all this"—Clawdy wiggled her fork toward the floor-to-ceiling windows that overlooked the explosion of color that comprised Los Angeles—"existed either. So ... why can't it work in reverse?"

"I'm not following," Venus said. Adam was thankful she had slowed her gorging before speaking.

"If I never knew all this existed, and yet it does, what about learning that something I thought existed *didn't*?"

"Are you saying you are doubting that Mother Dawn is real?" Mony asked.

The cyberpunks at the table fell silent in anticipation of the neuro-trancer's answer. They held their breaths, watching her stare out the windows at the expanse of the resplendent city colors beyond.

"It's time we tell them," Elvis muttered to the King of L.A. "We've added a frigging neuro-trancer to the equation. Do you even understand the ramifications of that?"

The King of L.A. sighed heavily and placed his white-bearded face into his hands.

"It's serendipity," Elvis continued. "It's the universe, not just *this* one but all of them, lining up to set *all* their worlds right."

"I know that," the assassin growled behind his hands, then raised his face to see Adam.

The cyberpunk felt uneasy for the first time in a while, with the way the assassin regarded him.

But the King of L.A. focused on Clawdy. "What brings a neuro-trancer out of the commune? What were you doing in the city?"

Adam studied Clawdy's face, intrigued at her answer and her story. Venus reached across the table and grabbed his hand. He smiled, feeling the warmth of her skin and again happy she was not dead.

"I wanted to bring trancing to the people, to those who couldn't get to the commune."

"And they let you go?" the King of L.A. asked, leaning back in his chair, folding his arms.

Clawdy glanced out the tall window again at the beautiful, colorful city that she never could have imagined existed, until she snapped her head back to focus on the table. "I ran." Then she fell silent and looked into her lap.

The cyberpunks, the assassin, and the barkeep respected her pause and waited for her to garner the courage to continue. Adam knew he was about to hear something unprecedented.

"I fled, is more like it. My mentor—lover, maybe—abused me. Scrambled my head with breaking the hard-and-fast rules we abide by. I couldn't take it anymore. Lost my faith." Clawdy glanced out the window again and spoke with her head turned. "Thought I could get it back if I brought Mother Dawn's message to the people, instead of always waiting for them to come to us."

Elvis let out an, "Oh boy," and scratched his forehead. "You do know Cyber-Corp would never have let you practice trancing outside the commune, right?"

The King of L.A. shot him a look.

Clawdy panned between the assassin and the barkeep, her brows furrowed in confusion. "What does Cyber-Corp have to do with neuro-trancers?"

Adam felt the tension at the table become palpable. Still holding Venus's hand, he squeezed it for reassurance—not necessarily for her benefit but to help settle his anxiety at the upcoming answer.

Elvis folded his hands and leaned forward on the table. He maintained focused eye contact with Clawdy when he asked, "Where do you think all the credits go from your customers who come for trancing?"

Clawdy's gaze darted back and forth between Elvis and the King of L.A. "I–I never thought about it."

"Don't you think"—Elvis shifted in his chair—"that you should have seen all those credits in your account?"

"I just assumed it went to the community pool of the commune."

The King of L.A.'s face changed from the softer, fatherly man, who he had portrayed with everyone recently, back to a hardened assassin. "Cyber-Corp has been taking all your credits for years. And you being off the commune and doing it freelance could expose them. Could expose"—he eyed Elvis and released a long exhale—"Mother Dawn."

"And that would *out* all the evil that makes them who they are. Basically using neuro-trancers as prostitutes. This is why they will hunt you until you are dead," Elvis said. "You were income to them. Now you are a threat. And keeping the ruse of Mother Dawn alive is income as well, but they need to neutralize the threat to the truth. *You.*"

Clawdy set her fork on her plate as if she were on autopilot. "I need to know what Mother Dawn is."

The King of L.A. and Elvis exchanged a look.

"Please …"

Doctor R appeared behind the King of L.A., panting, his shoulders bouncing with every labored breath. He leaned down and whispered in the assassin's ear for what felt like an eternity.

Adam side-eyed Venus and gave her a *What's going on* look. She shrugged, so he bounced his gaze between Jonesy and Mony to see if they could hear what the doctor was saying. His two friends shook their heads.

But the King of L.A.'s one good eye grew large, and he scooted his chair from the table a few inches. He curved his lips into his mouth and trapped some air in his cheeks, puffing them out.

Doctor R stood upright, and the King of L.A. focused on Clawdy. "Well, someone or something has destroyed the commune."

Clawdy frowned. "What do you mean, *destroyed?*"

"There was a raid on the property," Doctor R answered. "Just got intel from another cyberpunk cell on that side of the province."

Clawdy rose so fast that her chair skidded behind her and struck an empty chair from another table waiting for patrons. "What do you mean, *destroyed?*" she repeated.

Adam squeezed Venus's hand and looked at Jonesy, who had also grabbed Mony's hand for comfort.

"It appears"—the King of L.A. shook his head—"that you are the last living neuro-trancer."

011000011111000111011100

The King of L.A. entered his passcode into the keypad, and the blast door opened, exposing a large room of couches, recliner chairs, a desk, and tele-skins placed randomly, like modern art deco.

The four reunited cyberpunks, the last neuro-trancer, the one-eyed assassin, and the barkeep entered the large room. "I feel as if this is the setup of a bad joke," Elvis whispered to everyone behind him.

Venus couldn't help but chuckle, and Adam squeezed her in delight that she was here.

Jonesy and Mony walked to the far wall, spinning around to behold the massive room adorned in color and technology. Adam wondered if they would ever make a good couple—when all this was over. He wanted the best for his childhood friend, and who else would be worthy than a woman who had literally gone through hell with them?

"Find a comfy seat," the King of L.A. said. "Welcome to my office. We have lots to talk about."

Adam noticed, however, that the assassin did not take a comfy seat himself, rather he sat on the corner of his desk. Probably the most uncomfortable place to sit in the room. But the man was a hardened henchman, right? Even if Adam started to view him more as a father figure than a killer.

The King of L.A. sifted through large printouts of photographs while everyone in the room waited for him to speak. He sighed and looked up. "If you want to see the proof, this is what the cyberpunk cell sent us of the commune. Looks like the same bots that attacked us in the Peppermint Lounge also took out the commune." He made eye contact with Clawdy and glanced at her duffel bag at her feet as she sat on the lavender couch. "I won't ask you if you want the truth. I will just tell you the truth. And it might go against everything you thought. But that boy there"—he pointed at Adam—"is the candle, and you are the match."

Venus slipped her hand from Adam's and placed it on Clawdy's arm in reassurance.

Adam thought he should do something, should say something to ease Clawdy's anxiety, since just being in Los Angeles had turned his head upside down from what he had thought was real. But he understood the importance of her, as the last neuro-trancer and one who was already doubting Mother Dawn's existence, to hear the truth. "It was hard for me to hear, ma'am, but we are all on the same side here."

Clawdy nodded and directed her tear-stained eyes at the King of L.A.

"Good," the one-eyed assassin said. "Trancing isn't suicide or even death."

Adam noticed Clawdy tense up and watched Venus comfort her. Even though he had heard it before, Adam still listened intently as the King of L.A. explained again about the supercollider, the quantum computer, and how it created a new universe based on each of the colors of the properties of light—*Mother Dawn*, if you will.

"When someone is trancing," the King of L.A. continued, staring at the neuro-trancer, "they now exist outside Mother Dawn. What you call *Shangri-la* is really just experiencing the Big Bang of subatomic particles. Energy cannot be created nor destroyed, only changed, so the energy that makes up who you are gets transferred from Mother Dawn's mainframe into the collider, where, for a nanosecond, you see the origins of the universe as the collider recreates the Big Bang, before you become part of that energy and those subatomic particles forever."

Clawdy shook her head. "I'm wrestling with my faith, and I'm very aware of that, but Cain, my mentor, and so many others before him said Mother Dawn spoke to them."

Adam furrowed his brows and watched the King of L.A. to see how he would handle this new piece of information. Venus slipped a hand onto Adam's thigh, and he placed his hand atop hers.

The assassin pushed himself off his desk and paced the room, his hands clasped behind his back. "Let me guess …"

Adam noticed Elvis, who sat on a recliner in the corner, smirking. He also knew what the assassin was about to say. Adam inhaled deeply and grabbed Jonesy's wrist for comfort, just so happy his best friend was with him again. Then he shot Mony a look and a wink. That woman was something special.

The King of L.A. stopped pacing and glared at the last neuro-trancer. "Mother Dawn spoke to them in a series of tones, that *bing-binged* into a singular sound, with some static afterward."

Clawdy rose from the couch, as if she were a marionette. "Yes! How did you know?"

A knock sounded on the door.

"Come in," the assassin said.

The door opened, and a young woman in a lab coat rushed inside the office. "Sir, all our cameras have been knocked out."

Elvis rose from the recliner chair. "What do you mean, *knocked out?*"

The woman looked at him. "All our screens are black. We can't see anything outside the dome."

Elvis eyed the King of L.A. but instructed the woman, "Check the power grid. If that looks okay, send a few scouts on shock-riders."

"Yes, sir." She gave a half bow and exited the office.

Everyone inside the room remained silent, no one wanting to be the first to speak or to add more chaos to the situation with questions.

The King of L.A. bit his thumb's fingernail, which did not sit right with Adam. Something was wrong; he had never seen the assassin this distressed. Then the man pursed his lips and squinted at the neuro-trancer. "The tone they all heard was mirroring a modem dial-up. That was the inception of computers being able to talk online. Mother Dawn, the computer, used the sound progression of the modem from the 1990s as a language to communicate with computers here. She normally uses qubits to compute. Way faster than anything we can track."

"So, she adopted the original and slowest way to talk to us here," Adam finished. "That way we could understand her?"

"No, not *us*." The King of L.A. regarded Clawdy. "It was so the neuro-trancers could understand her. She was speaking to them in the most primitive version of computing's morse code—the modem dial-up *ping ping* sound. And they all fell for it."

0110000011111000111011100

The King of L.A. held open the door so all his guests could exit the room into the hallway. When everyone had left, he stepped out himself. "All right. Follow me to the control center. I want to see what's up with the camera blackouts, and we can finish talking there." He focused on Adam when he said the last part.

They entered the dome-shaped control room, full of workers in lab coats manning the consoles, and Adam smirked when he saw Venus, Jonesy, and the neuro-trancer gaze around with childlike wonder.

"Pretty amazing, *huh?*" he said quietly to Venus, nudging her side with his elbow.

"Who would have thought that a city, full of so many colors and so many anti-implanters, existed right under our noses." Venus stepped forward, staring at the tele-skins.

"Any update on the external cameras?" the King of L.A. asked one technician, leaning over her shoulder to see her console readouts.

"Power grid is fully operational. We've sent a team of five shock-riders into the wastelands to see if anything is interfering with the transmissions."

Adam watched the King of L.A. stand upright, inhale, and hold his breath. He didn't like the assassin's demeanor. Something was off.

The King of L.A. faced the four cyberpunks and the neuro-trancer. Elvis had moved to a console to track the shock-riders. The assassin sucked in his lips and glared at Adam. He approached the boy and Clawdy, then kneeled in front of them so that he looked upward at them.

This did not make Adam feel better. What an uncharacteristic gesture for the assassin to make. Adam felt Venus's arms wrap around him from behind for support.

"The quantum computer—called Mother Dawn," the King of L.A. began, glancing at Clawdy to ensure she was listening, "works on absolutes." He refocused on Adam. "If we can get you back to the mainframe—since this version of you is not supposed to exist in this reality—back to the Big Bang of *your* universe, it will disrupt Mother Dawn's stability, making her vulnerable, like a weapon disabling a forcefield. That will give us the window to bypass her kill switch, delete the code regarding the implants, and hopefully make them inoperable across *all* universes."

Venus grabbed Adam's hand in a death grip. "Wait. What are you saying? You want Adam to sacrifice himself?"

She inadvertently looked at the neuro-trancer. "You want him to voluntarily go through trancing?"

The King of L.A. rubbed his white beard and inhaled deeply. "Trancing will act like sticking a tree branch into a bike spoke. It will jam Mother Dawn for enough time to expose the kill switch code that Mr. Broad inserted, and we can override all the evil Cyber-Corp has done. Not just here in this universe but across all of them."

Venus spun around Adam's body, grabbed him by the waist, and pleaded with her eyes. "You can't do this. I can't lose you! We can keep fighting here. Stick with the plan."

Adam had used every ounce of energy and courage to take his gaze from the woman he loved and raise it to meet the assassin's eyes.

"Isn't this what you cyberpunks are fighting for in the first place—what *all* us freedom fighters are sacrificing ourselves for? You hold the key, Adam, to not just win the battle but to win the war that you completely pledged yourself to win."

What the King of L.A. had just said resonated so deeply within Adam's core that he couldn't ignore the message.

"But …" Venus said. "But not like this. We can take them down from the inside."

Jonesy rubbed the back of his head and released the loudest, most aggravated grunt Adam had ever heard from his best friend. "I hate this. Every single piece of it." He made eye contact with Venus. "But the old guy is right. We have been willing to sacrifice ourselves for the cause since we were old enough to walk. We've been with the very person who has the ability to take it all down. This is what we wanted."

Adam tilted his head at his best friend, wondering how he had come to terms with the plan so easily.

"I won't do it," a female voice said from behind the cyberpunks.

They had forgotten about the neuro-trancer.

"It's not how we do trancing. This feels like a whole bunch of conspiracy *poo-do* if you ask me. If the boy has any reservations about trancing, I refuse."

Elvis closed his eyes and pinched the bridge of his nose. "I don't think you guys understand the ramifications of what we are sitting on right now. If Adam goes through trancing—with the last neuro-trancer known on the planet—it will scramble the main computer just long enough for us to destroy the code that Cyber-Corp wrote into *all* the universes." He ran his tongue along his top teeth and focused on Adam. "You won't just be saving this universe from the megacorporations. You'll be resetting the government for all eight realities and sending Cyber-Corp to the ground. In *all* realities. This is so much bigger than you ever thought, when you were hiding in the subway and wanting to take out a single factory. You will be freeing every single universe."

Venus closed her eyes and pushed her whole face into Adam's chest. "There's got to be another way."

Red lights spun as a blaring alarm sounded in the control room.

"Sir," one of the lab coats said, peering over their shoulder at the King of L.A. "Something just blew up the mirage dome, and whatever it was, is now entering Los Angeles. And there's a lot of them."

41

Mr. Broad wrung his hands in anticipation as he and Johnny Ray watched the massive tele-skin in his office. Rows and rows of slavebots—a platoon—had reached the mirage dome. Mr. Broad switched the view on the monitor from the drone above and to the lead bot. Now watching from ground level, Mr. Broad instructed Lancelot to give the command for the front row of the slavebot army to stick the mortars in the desert sand, against the mirage dome.

The image on the screen approached the dome, then dipped as the slavebot lowered itself, and Mr. Broad watched the robotic hands wiggle a rectangular explosive with two metal stakes into the ground. Then the bot stood upright.

"Lancelot, have the front row move backward to the rest of the platoon for detonation."

"Yes, sir."

Mr. Broad quickly jumped from camera to camera inside the front row of slavebots' eyes to ensure all had moved to a safe distance. "Blow it open. Everyone dies but the boy."

"Very good, sir."

The tele-skin flashed orange for a split second as all the mortars exploded at once. Mr. Broad dialed up the lead slavebot's camera and watched, from the comfort of his office, dozens of his robotic army fire clipper rounds at anything and everything that moved.

The slavebots spread wide into the Los Angeles streets, littering pedestrians—men, women, children, pets—with clipper rounds. Gunfire riddled vehicles with holes as people screamed, dropped to the ground, or ran. Cars skidded and crashed into buildings, other people, and other vehicles.

Fireballs of explosions plumed almost in a symphonic crescendo. One, BOOM, two, BOOM, three, BOOM—as the slavebots desecrated the streets. Parents draped themselves over their dead children as they screamed for help. Usually the bot would hear the screams for help, then kill those people within seconds.

Pedestrians and people who had abandoned their vehicles fled from the scene, only to have a barrage of clipper rounds mow them down from behind. Dead bodies of all ages fell—some decapitated, some with limbs tens of feet from their torsos. The ones whose fate was worse were the ones still alive, with their innards spilling from their bellies, as they screeched in pain.

"Lancelot?"

"Yes, sir?"

"Scan for the two Synchestria Implants."

Lancelot stayed silent as he had the lead slavebot scan Los Angeles for Venus and Jonesy. Then he said, "They are together in a building."

"Probably with the rest of the brats. Have the slavebots set their coordinates for that location. No prisoners this time. And no mercy."

"Very good, sir."

Clipper rounds filled the air like horizontal rain, until the slavebots formed perfect ranks, holstering their weapons. As they marched toward the Concrete Kingdom, they had to step over the dead in the streets and on the sidewalk.

42

The building shook, and the King of L.A. instinctively grabbed Adam and Venus so they wouldn't tumble to the metal-grated floor. When he got his footing, he stumbled toward a console to have the technician switch to the cameras that monitored the closest streets inside the mirage dome.

The cyberpunks, Clawdy, Elvis, and Doctor R came alongside the King of L.A. to watch the screens. Mony gasped and threw a palm over her open mouth to prevent making any further noise as the team watched those same robotic soldiers infiltrate the street, systematically killing any human who moved.

Venus squeaked and dug her face into Adam's chest, unable to watch the unbiased clipper rounds as they cut children in half. The image of pandemonium on the screens just couldn't match the level of violence that was actually occurring for these people.

"Oh, Mother Dawn," Clawdy whispered beside Jonesy and grabbed for his hand in comfort.

"They know where we are," the King of L.A. said, turning to the group behind him, eyes wide. "They're following your implant signals. It'll lead them right to us."

Venus pulled her head from Adam's chest, her cheeks stained in tears. "Then we gotta get our implants out."

"We don't have time," the assassin answered.

"Nor the resources to do it safely," Doctor R added.

"We gotta get them out!" Venus clawed at her neck, digging her fingernails into her skin, trying to rip them from her body herself.

Adam grabbed her arm before she really hurt herself.

"We gotta get them out!" Her hair flailed like a storm as she shook her head, still gouging her skin with her nails. "We gotta get them out!" Her panicked voice was ear-piercing.

The King of L.A. grabbed her free hand while Adam remained latched on to Venus's other arm. Adam spun her so he could wrap his arms around her in a bear hug, trapping her arms against his body, rendering them useless.

"Listen, babe. That's not gonna help. You can't remove them yourself. They already know where we are."

"Then we run," Jonesy said, absentmindedly rubbing the spot on his neck where the implant resided.

"The bots are machines," the King of L.A. said. "We would need to stop to eat or to sleep. They don't need to. We would survive one day, maybe two, before they ran us through."

Venus pushed herself from Adam's embrace and stared into his ice-blue eyes. "Then we run. Just me and Jonesy." Her gaze landed on Mony, then the King of L.A., then Clawdy, then Elvis and Doctor R. "They will only follow us. They can only track *us*." She narrowed her eyes at Jonesy so he understood the ramifications of what she was implying. "We run, until we can't run anymore. Draw them away from here. Keep the rest of you safe and … alive."

Jonesy's eyes widened, and he swallowed hard when he realized she meant for them to sacrifice themselves for the betterment of the group.

The King of L.A. nudged Venus aside to step in front of Adam and to grab the cyberpunk by both his shoulders. "We only have one possible solution," he said to the boy.

Behind them, all the monitors showed a temporary ceasefire of the robotic army. Its initial carnage may be over, yet the bot army marched in perfect rhythm toward the Concrete Kingdom.

Adam blinked in rapid succession and glanced at Venus as she wiped her tear-stained eyes with her sleeve.

The assassin spoke. "You must return to Mother Dawn. You and only you can disrupt the kill switch so we can remove Cyber-Corp from her programming." The King of L.A. held Adam's shoulders. As he regarded Clawdy, he added, "And only trancing can end this. For good."

Clawdy stepped backward and placed a hand over her heart, shaking her head. "Oh, Mother Dawn, no. I ... couldn't."

Venus screamed and shoved away the King of L.A. so she could hug Adam. "You can't leave me!"

Adam swallowed hard and kissed the top of her head. "Babe, you were ready to sacrifice yourself for me just a minute ago. How is this any different?"

With her face smothered in his chest and her voice muffled, she said, "Because there is still a slight chance I live. Trancing is ... instant death."

Adam kissed her head again and brought her in tighter.

"It also instantly saves the world from Cyber-Corp," Elvis reiterated.

"No, not just this world," the King of L.A. clarified. "Adam, remember that by doing this, you are removing Cyber-Corp from *all* seven color universes, as well as mine— the full-color main reality."

Adam glanced at the monitors and saw the robot army wasn't very far from the Concrete Kingdom. They would descend upon the building shortly.

"I won't let you go," Venus said, Adam's chest still muffling her voice.

The King of L.A. cupped the side of Adam's cheek like a parent. "Boy, isn't this what you've been fighting for since you could remember? Isn't *this* why you became a cyberpunk? Isn't *this* the whole reason for every move, every thought, every plan you've ever had? To take down Cyber-Corp and to restore the governments, to bring order and peace back to the country? With this one selfless act, you will accomplish that. Here. And in the other universes. Plus in the main reality. A true cyberpunk warrior."

"The most revered warrior. The one who saved the future of so many universes," Elvis added.

"You can't leave me," Venus sobbed.

Adam took a deep breath, held it, and exhaled slowly and loudly. He lowered his cheek to the top of Venus's head and murmured, "I would be a hypocrite if I didn't do this …"

0110000011111000111011100

The Concrete Kingdom rocked on its foundation as slavebots unleashed their firepower at the front doors. The King of L.A. grabbed the headrest of the chair nearest to him to keep his balance. The lights in the building shut off, to save energy. Meanwhile, the backup generators kicked on to supply the building with minimal power.

Adam clung to Venus tighter to prevent her from toppling over.

"We gotta get into one of the panic rooms," Doctor R said. "Now!"

The technicians in lab coats scrambled from their consoles to head through the door, abandoning their posts.

The King of L.A. outstretched his arms wide behind his group to herd them together. They followed a step behind the doctor and out the control room door.

Clawdy fell back a bit so that she walked alongside the King of L.A. "When this is all over, I would like for you to tell me the truth. Every piece of it."

"Even if it disagrees with everything you've believed?" the assassin asked.

They traversed the corridor, with sounds of clipper rounds and explosions—and people's screams—behind them and a few floors down.

"*Especially* if it does." The neuro-trancer eyed him, readjusting her duffel bag onto her shoulder. "I've felt something was … off for a while now, and I couldn't put my finger on it."

When an explosion rocked the corridor, the group ducked reflexively. The slavebots were getting closer, annihilating anything that moved in their wake.

The King of L.A. scanned the heads of his troupe to ensure everyone was still okay and accounted for. He told the neuro-trancer, "Ya know, maybe … just maybe, you always had a larger calling and didn't know it. Just as Adam has also."

The slavebots now breeched the control room floor behind them. The neuro-trancer frowned at the assassin in confusion and uncertainty, even as they ran, squatting to make themselves less of a target.

"Maybe Mother Dawn picked you, Clawdy. I don't think it's coincidence that you, of all people, are now the last neuro-trancer and the one to be the catalyst to perform the last trancing to set everything right in *all* the worlds. All of them, Clawdy. Not just here. You will become not just the last but *the* neuro-trancer for all the ages."

"Parise Mother Dawn," she whispered just loud enough for the assassin to hear her, and he smiled.

Ahead, Doctor R had stopped at an open door, waving the group through it and into a room. The King of L.A. did a silent head count as he watched each enter the darkness beyond: Adam, Venus, Mony, Jonesy. Then he, Clawdy, and Elvis entered next. All accounted for.

Doctor R was the last one in, now that everyone was safely inside the dark room. He closed the door with a *clang*. He turned on the light to expose a thick metal door, still open inside the room, and the doctor closed that door against the first door he had shut. The inside of the door, facing the room, had a large metal wheel that he turned clockwise, until a loud *click* reverberated through the room.

"I don't know of anything that can penetrate those two doors," Doctor R said, panting and out of breath.

Even though the sounds of clipper rounds, explosions, and people screaming got closer, it remained muffled from behind the double panic room doors.

Adam quickly surveyed the area—a few cots, a cabinet with glass doors revealing shelves of canned food, and sealed buckets stacked from floor to ceiling with WATER printed on the side.

"How long do you think we'll be in here?" Mony asked.

The King of L.A. stared at her for a beat before answering. "Only as long as it takes Adam to decide to go through with the trancing."

Venus squeaked out a sob before catching it.

"Once he does, Cyber-Corp will fall, and those bots out there will either disappear—blink out of existence, as if they never were invented in the first place—or just become inoperable and die on the spot."

"Wait," Adam said, stepping forward. "You don't know what will happen if I go through with the trancing?"

"Not exactly," Elvis answered. "We just know that you returning to the mainframe will allow us to remove the Cyber-Corp code. Maybe that means none of this actually happened, and none of you will remember any of this happening or will remember Adam ever existing. Maybe Cyber-Corp will just disappear, keeping everyone aware of what happened. Memories intact."

"I don't want to forget you," Venus said and laid her head on Adam's shoulder.

"I'll never forget you, mate," Jonesy said, with a crooked smile. "They can't take that away from us."

Adam nodded.

The panic room trembled as rounds and explosives hit the first metal door that separated them from the slavebots and certain death.

"Let's go, son," the King of L.A. said. "Everything you've done in your life has prepared you for this moment. Every citizen is relying on you to do the right thing, without realizing it, for their increased quality of life—and the quality of life for countless generations to come."

Adam made eye contact with the neuro-trancer and spied her duffel bag. He pulled Venus from his body and gave her the warmest smile he could muster. "We both know it's not only the right thing to do but it's the only way to win this war."

She nodded. "I'll never forget you."

"I know." Adam kissed her forehead.

"And I'll never stop loving you."

Adam pulled an item from his back pocket. With the object hidden in his fist, he grabbed Venus's wrist and made her open her hand. He placed in her palm the trinket he had found during their railway car raid, the night before all hell broke loose on their little group—when Maggie and Cherie were still alive. "If you ever start to doubt why I had to do this, take this to remind yourself what we were fighting for, from the very beginning." He closed her fingers around the fidget spinner.

A sob spurted from her nose, and she chuckled in embarrassment. She wiped her nose with her sleeve, then planted a long, firm kiss on his lips. "Go save all the universes. The public may never know what you did for them, but I'll always know you were the real hero."

"We all are heroes, Venus. Even the ones we lost along the way."

She nodded and stepped aside.

Adam was startled to see that Clawdy had already set up her trancing station on one of the cots.

The barrage of gunfire and explosions outside the room remained relentless.

"They know we're in here," the King of L.A. said, "because of those blasted implants. They think they've checkmated us. I wish I could see the look on Mr. Broad's face when all this goes to hell for him."

Adam laid on the coat, crossed his feet at the ankles, and eyed Clawdy. "Does it hurt?"

The neuro-trancer smiled in reassurance. "I … don't really know. No one has ever come back to describe it."

With that, Venus choked out another sob.

Clawdy pulled a syringe with the orange liquid from her duffel bag. "It will be quick. Do you have any last things you want to say?"

Adam rose onto one elbow and scanned the faces in front of him—a ragtag team who should not be working together so well. "Take care of yourselves. And each other." Then he plopped into a lying position.

"Do you want to be hypnotized?" Clawdy asked him.

She had briefed him on the mandated beginning to any trancing session, and he replied, "Yes."

Everyone faced the door when the sound of destruction suddenly ceased from the other side. The King of L.A. didn't know if the silence from the attacking bots should concern him or should set his mind at ease.

From the corner of his eye, Adam saw Jonesy wrap an arm around Venus. Adam's heart rate accelerated with nervousness as to what lay on the other side, and he tried to calm his nerves with questions. *I wonder what will happen to all the implants inside all the people. What will happen to the 3-11 Men now that their services aren't needed anymore? Will they come out from the shadows to find real jobs? And what will happen to all the families who relied on the income from the Synchestria Implants? Will they now go hungry? Homeless?* He hadn't considered that taking down Cyber-Corp might ruin millions of families forever, sending them into poverty and destitution.

He panicked for half a second, wanting to call it off so they could discuss the ramifications further, but that was all the time he had left to formulate any regrets.

The last neuro-trancer had already pushed the plunger of the trancing syringe.

43

Mr. Broad and Johnny Ray watched the tele-skin, their postures ramrod straight. The monitor showed plumes of smoke and clipper rounds finding the backs of the fleeing people inside the Concrete Kingdom. The slavebots casually stepped over all the dead on their march closer to where the two signals from the cyberpunks' implants came from.

"They can't run forever." Mr. Broad watched the two orange markers move down a corridor, away from the slavebots.

Johnny Ray took a casual sip from his glass, swallowed, and pointed to the screen. "They stopped moving. They went inside that room."

"Lancelot," Mr. Broad said.

"Yes, sir?"

"Have a slavebot scan the properties of that room where our two marks entered and stopped."

"Right away, sir." A moment passed, and Lancelot's electronic male voice filled the office. "It's comprised of tungsten."

Mr. Broad snickered. "Someone would only ever use tungsten for one reason to design a room. It's a safe room."

Johnny Ray asked, "Lancelot?"

"Yes, sir?"

"Do you see any other entrances or exits to that safe room?"

"Sir, it appears only one portal exists for that room."

Johnny Ray was smiling so wide when he took his next sip of spirits that some liquid spilled from the corners of his mouth. "No reason to waste ammunition or battery life, right?"

Mr. Broad nodded.

"Lancelot?"

"Yes, sir?"

"Have the slavebots form ranks down the hallway in front of that door. Then put them in standby mode."

"Very good, sir."

"They can stay like that for all eternity, for all I care," Johnny Ray mumbled. Then a bit louder, he added, "Time is on our side. We just wait. Even if it's a month until they run out of supplies inside that safe room, they'll eventually have to crack open the door for *something*."

"Lancelot," Mr. Broad said.

"Yes, sir?"

"Program the slavebots to come out of standby mode and to engage as soon as that door's latch is unlocked."

"Very good, sir." A moment of silence passed. "They have been instructed."

The tele-skins revealed a calm scene. No rising smoke. No clipper rounds filling the air. No screams or people falling to the floor with holes in their backs. The slavebots, heads lolled forward, were now quiet and motionless.

"Lancelot?" Mr. Broad asked.

Nothing.

"Lancelot?"

Nothing.

"*Lancelot?*"

Nothing.

Mr. Broad eyed Johnny Ray and squinted in confusion. He approached his desk and typed *cmd* on the keyboard. The tele-skin covering the far wall turned black, and an orange cursor blinked in the top left corner.

Johnny Ray watched the letters form on the tele-skin as Mr. Broad typed from the keyboard: *lancelot.exe*, then took another sip of his drink.

Mr. Broad hit Enter. "Lancelot?"

Still nothing.

Mr. Broad glanced behind him at Johnny Ray and swallowed hard. "I'm going to reboot the whole system."

Johnny Ray nodded and shifted his weight from one foot to the other.

Mr. Broad hunched over his keyboard, and Johnny Ray watched the tele-skin as his boss typed again. On the screen, the orange cursor moved as it formed the command *shutdown /r.*

The owner of Cyber-Corp in this universe looked back at his assistant one more time before he executed the command.

Johnny Ray nodded for him to try it, to see what happens. "If we're offline, that's the only thing to do."

"I know, but *why* are we offline?" Mr. Broad asked, concern dripping in his tone. "Something doesn't feel right."

Johnny Ray casually sipped again from his glass and wiped his lips with the back of his hand. "What's the worst that could happen?"

Mr. Broad's finger hovered over the Enter button. "Losing every piece of data that we've collected is the worst that could happen. And that's pretty bad, if you ask me." He took a deep breath, steeled himself to push the Enter key, and lowered his finger toward the button.

Behind him, Mr. Broad heard Johnny's Ray glass of liquor hit the floor before he heard his assistant's body crumple to the floor also. He turned, just as his own legs and muscles betrayed him, his body on the way to the floor as well. Yet he caught a glimpse of what had happened.

The office became narrower in Mr. Broad's vision as he struck the floor, and he noticed Johnny Ray's eyes were closed. The man wasn't moving. Mr. Broad felt pins and needles explode throughout every fiber of his being. And the room became even smaller.

He couldn't open his mouth—he had lost all control of his body—never mind to scream or to make any noise. From where his head landed on his office floor, his eyes were in line to see the massive tele-skin that covered the back wall.

The blinking orange cursor at the end of the reboot prompt became solid, then reversed, deleting the command that Mr. Broad had typed. His vision continued to narrow as he lost consciousness.

The last thing he saw before he disappeared from this universe was the orange cursor typing the words, *By the people, for the people* ...

44

The King of L.A. pushed open the top of the empathy machine from a lying position inside, like a vampire opening a coffin's lid, until the cover locked into place straight up. He gripped the sides of the machine and sat upright. He removed the vantablack goggles from his face and used his knuckles to rub his eyes. The machine had four thick cables running from it, each sprouting from the four corners and running into the quantum computer on the other side of the room—Mother Dawn herself.

"Welcome back, Gene," said the man in the suit, standing alongside his assistant and two armed guards.

"Thank you, Mr. President. Mission accomplished." The King of L.A. shook his head to clear the cobwebs of the months he had just spent inside the empathy machine to visit the Orange Reality. He grabbed a neatly folded pile of clean clothes, dressed his naked body, then stepped from the box. He laid the goggles onto the metal tray next to the quantum computer.

"Your service and devotion to the United States of America will not go unnoticed. Neither by my administration nor future ones. You truly have saved and preserved the governments of our reality, as well as the seven light realities, from evil."

"I appreciate that, Mr. President." The King of L.A. bent over and placed his palms on his thighs to prepare for a series of coughs and dry heaves that always come from extended times inside the empathy machine—inside the other universes.

"Gene, we have a full recovery program set up for you," the president said. He approached the King of L.A. and placed a hand on his shoulder while the scientist's chest racked a series of coughs. "Massages. Saunas. Bottomless buffets. You deserve to be pampered after all this."

The King of L.A. chuckled through his hacking. "Just a nap will suffice, Mr. President. Can we confirm that the Cyber-Corp code was deleted from the mainframe before I go relax?"

"You actually got that boy to do it. To sacrifice his life to save all the universes."

"The trick wasn't getting him to agree, Mr. President. The trick was finding him and keeping him alive long enough to convince him to go through with it."

A technician in a lab coat, similar to those in the Concrete Kingdom's control room, turned from a monitor. "I don't see the code anywhere in Mother Dawn. It's not showing up in the individual coding for the seven light realities either."

"What do you think happened to Cyber-Corp when the neuro-trancer sent the boy trancing?" the president asked the King of L.A. while smoothing his tie against his button-down shirt.

"This is unprecedented. I don't want to create false rumors with my speculation."

The president laughed. "Why wouldn't I expect anything less from you, Gene?"

The King of L.A. felt weird, after being in the light realities for so long, to have someone call him by his first name and not by his handle. For the first time, it made him uncomfortable. He had started to truly own the King of L.A. moniker.

"Mr. President, we need to leave," one of the secret service agents said, pushing on an earpiece to listen better. "You'll be late."

Gene raised an eyebrow at the president.

"Ah, yes. Tonight is the first presidential debate. I forget that you were over there for so long this time."

Gene—the King of L.A.—scratched his white beard and ran a hand through his thinning hair. "So, who got their nomination?"

The president checked his phone and clacked away while answering a message. "Ray Broadman." He twirled his finger in the air to signal to his agents that they were to leave. "We'll catch up, Gene. Good work, as always. Godspeed."

The King of L.A. felt the blood drain from his face. The door closed behind the President of the United States, leaving the scientist/assassin in Mother Dawn's control room with a technician.

Ray Broadman.

Johnny *Ray*.

Mr. *Broad*.

The King of L.A. stared wide-eyed at the Mother Dawn computer and the supercollider beyond it and whispered to no one in particular, "My God, what have we done?"

011000011111000111011100

Thank you for reading *Tomorrow People*.
Would you take a moment leave a review?